PERFECT SON

A Lynzee Rose Mystery

Victoria Walters, Author

WESTBOW
PRESS
A DIVISION OF THOMAS NELSON

First in the Lynzee Rose Mystery Series

This book is a work of fiction. All characters, organizations, and events are the products of the author's imagination or used fictiously.

WestBow Press books may be ordered through booksellers or by contacting:

WestBow Press
A Division of Thomas Nelson
1663 Liberty Drive
Bloomington, IN 47403
www.westbowpress.com
1-(866) 928-1240

ISBN: 978-1-4497-2949-3 (sc)
ISBN: 978-1-4497-2950-9 (hc)
ISBN: 978-1-4497-2948-6 (e)

Library of Congress Control Number: 2011918513

Printed in the United States of America

WestBow Press rev. date: 1/2/2013

For my dearest friend, Lela Watson, whose shared love of a great mystery gave birth to this one. And for my newly discovered cousin, Geri Redmond, editor and enthusiast.

Special Acknowledgement
To My Son and Story Developer Supreme,
Seth Michael Williamson

INTRODUCTION

FRIDAY, MAY 20TH

One bizarre theory of the origin of Mima Mounds, pronounced "Mima" (MY-ma), is the northwestern Pocket Gopher. These potato-sized creatures were said to have created the Mounds over generations of frantic territorial construction.

Over thirty other theories attempt to explain the Mounds ranging from ancient fish nests to asteroid impacts. In actuality, they are prairie lands full of thousands of closely packed *'Mounds of Mystery'* with as many ongoing theories as to their origin as there are mounds.

Found only in limited areas in the United States, the primary mound-bearing prairies of the Puget Lowlands lie in the prairie lands of Thurston County, Washington. They are the nation's best example of the unusual phenomena. Today Mima Mounds Preserve included something more unusual . . . . . a new mound.

CHAPTER 1

SATURDAY, MAY 21ST

"Lynzee, meet me ASAP. Body. Probably not by natural causes. I want you in on it from the get go. I have the go ahead from the higher ups. Soon as you can, then."

My lack of response clued him in he may have missed something.

"Sorry to be so short. Lack of Sleep. I should have first asked if you are available to do some more work for us before I start ordering you around. Are you?"

Better, I thought. "I appreciate the consideration, Carl. Tell me what you have, and we'll go from there." I listened as he rolled out a two-minute summary of his past twenty-four hours, and something about '*ruffled feathers*' when I'd heard enough.

"I'm in. On my way."

The snap of his cell phone ended the call. One of Chief Deputy Detective Watson's many skills did not include the art of conversation, at least the two way kind. A man of few words, our brief exchange informed me of a discovery at one of earth's strangest landscapes located in the humble prairies twelve miles south of my home in Olympia, Washington. The remains of a young man have been discovered.

1

I dressed quickly to the hum of the morning news and aroma of freshly brewing coffee, the latter brewed with a hint of caramel today. The fragrance followed me around all four hundred square feet of my studio sized home as I rushed about making myself presentable. Today, that entailed passing a brush through my hair, a toothbrush over my teeth, and soap and water across my face.

Carl, my friend and part-time employer, asked me to meet him at Mima Mounds, located in the middle of nowhere. One never knows what to expect in the middle of nowhere; so, I packed accordingly. I filled my coffee thermos, threw in a bottle of water, and packed a sandwich.

Gathering up what the predicted forecast assured me I would need, a light jacket for a cooler than expected late May day, I added an umbrella, having little trust in anyone whose job security isn't based on performance. In the maritime climate of Western Washington, summers are cool and winters wet, or is it the other way around? Realistically, all twelve months are the same. Wet. I live in an area referred to as '*Puget Sound*', technically the name of a body of water, but the rains fall so much here, the distinction gets lost.

When I pulled into the visitor parking lot, the clock on the dash read nine. I rolled down the window. The crispness felt fresh but chilly. A canopy of Douglas fir, overhead, was out of place in the surrounding prairie land and added to the coolness of the morning.

I spotted a restroom and lectured myself. 'Better do it now, Lynzee. It's not going to go away by itself. You're the one who had to drink the whole thermos of coffee on the ride down. Okay', again to myself, 'I better go.' I rolled the window up and locked the car. Hurrying back from the minimal facilities, I started the car and fired up the heat to get warm again.

My candy apple red Transit was like a beacon; out of place in this *au natural* setting. Ecological correctness won over. I turned off the engine and watched for a signal from Carl.

Thinking of the many theories of how Mima Mounds were

formed, I remembered first becoming aware of them a decade ago. However, it was making out with a long ago work mate, Jim, in the parking lot I remember most.

From the expansive entrance, the Mounds look like a sea of giant buried bowling balls, reminding me of an old folk tale about a man who slept for forty years and wakes to the sound of crashing ninepins.

These little hills became a part of the region's history when Charles Wilkes, leader of the expedition charting the Pacific Northwest, happened upon them in the mid eighteen hundreds. Thinking they were Native American burial sites with hidden treasure, he destroyed many, finding only earth inside. History doesn't focus on this hideous act of their travels.

Geologists and other experts provide dozens of hypotheses and theories of glacial freeze-and-thaw cycles, erosion, interplay between wind and vegetation, an earthquake or two, or perhaps a volcanic eruption.

My vote and favorite is the alien theory. I'm not alone.

Local folklore, too, offers a solution by way of a giant of a Northwest logger, Paul Bunyan. It goes something like this: When Paul dug out Puget Sound he created the Mounds. But, the 'why' or even the 'how' is missing for this theory to hold more than Paul's Puget waters. Local lore also promotes a magic angle to these little hills, declaring that if you try to flatten them, they mysteriously reappear.

The debate continues. However, you tell the story of the existence of these mounds, one of these mounds didn't belong here, and never did. From what I learned this morning, the Mounds was about to make news again, this time as the scene of a major crime.

My degrees in behavioral science and counseling, combined with a career as a mediator, opened up this new world of problem solving. A world outside the confines of a safe environment, my conference room. On a normal day, my world involves an issue-based process producing a result all parties can live with…best case scenario…

win-win. Yet, here I am. A place where no possibility of negotiating exists. Death settled the matter.

The landscape, aching to bloom into a summer still weeks away, changed in front of my eyes as the sun pulled up over the Mounds like a blanket. Coming up on thirty minutes since I drove in, my thermos was empty, and my sack lunch was calling my name. I shivered. It would be noon before I shed my jacket. About to dig into my sandwich, I saw movement out the windshield.

Carl walked toward my direction. His tall slender build confessing that he was particular about what he ate. He was particular about many things, some of which including being determined, detached, dedicated, and, my least favorite, disciplined. My presence is due to another of those qualities, detail oriented, which sometimes includes the addition of my wider perspective approach, landing me on the County payroll from time to time.

Expressionless except for his lips pursed in his perpetual Mona Lisa smile, Carl raised an arm gesturing for me to come forward.

I exited my warm place and headed his way. Several others joined him, no one I immediately recognized. They stared at their feet as I approached, a frequent occurrence when I appear on a scene. I may be a sanctioned partner in the Thurston County Sheriff's Department, but I remain a curiosity to officials who either won their positions in local elections or received their appointments because they helped those who were elected. The air felt tense. I decided *not* to offer my theory on Mima Mounds just now.

The County Coroner appeared from behind me, nodding in my direction, offering a muttered apology for the slight jolt as he passed by. His semi-stooped posture had the characteristic look of someone standing over an autopsy table for most of their adult life. His disheveled appearance confirmed my suspicion; he'd been here all night.

"No problem, Doctor," I said as he passed. I forget his name. Part of my mediator training included keeping my focus *off* names and *on* problem solving. Names bring long forgotten personal memory association into the carefully structured neutral environment that mediation requires. Unfortunately, all those years of forgetting names have carried over into my private life.

Carl began making the introductions, awkwardly. "This is my Investigations Consultant, Lynzee Rose." Eyebrows rising like the wave in a football stadium.

Among the group, he pointed out a photographer intern from a local college, the Park Ranger who found the body, and the Thurston County Commissioner who lives in nearby Littlerock. I remember seeing this Commissioner on the news not long ago. Something about tribal fishing rights. Thinking back to Wilkes' obsession with Indian burial grounds, the fact she is a member of the Nisqually Indian Tribe might have some bearing on her presence today.

We exchanged contact numbers all around. I wanted to say 'thanks for having me' in some way that made sense at a crime scene. But, I was at a loss for the right words, so I smiled and nodded my hellos. Great. I have to come up with an appropriate crime scene greeting.

Commissioner Heather Whittier gave a slight nod in my direction and left with a cell phone pressed tightly against her ear. This scene spoke badly for the upcoming tourism season that keeps so many little towns across Washington alive for another year.

Ranger Dan Freis removed himself from the group muttering something about changing jobs.

The photographer intern, whose name I didn't register, made his excuses; and, holding his camera up as proof of purpose, took off, he said, to develop his film.

"More cuts in the budget, Carl?" I mused as he shuffled his feet from side to side. The group now down to the two of us, I smirked up at him.

Standing at six feet- two inches tall, shuffling his size twelve's without tripping over them in the process was no easy task. "Yeah, we gotta take what we can get where we can get it. Kid's a friend of my neighbor. Has a dream of going to work for CNN."

Cuts in the County budget, due to this serious economic climate, are no joking matter. Carl prided himself on a professional operation. His daily battles to keep department dollars from the budget trimmers ate into his street time. What I know about the cuts made to public safety budget cuts scares me more than a clown at my door on Halloween.

My own mediation career has been taking a hard hit these days; people choosing to live with their problems rather than part with their money.

Getting myself back to the business at hand, I said, "I meant the lack of crime scene investigators and the like." I did a slow turn around to emphasize my brilliant deductive powers of observation.

"I'll get to that," his few words on the matter. Looking outward into the Mounds from where we stood on one of several interpretive trails, Carl addressed himself, seemingly, to a particular mound. "Hey, Bob. You about done?"

Ah, now it came to me. Dr. Robert Wilson, Thurston County Coroner, going on twenty years in an elected position. That says something about the man or about his constituency anyway.

Standing up, he stepped to one side of a mound, coming into view. Hands cupped to his mouth, he yelled out to increase his volume over the distance between us, "Yeah, well, this is some kind of …in all my years," was all I caught for his effort. Collecting his equipment and his thoughts, Dr. Bob came toward us scribbling in his infamous notebook. Rumor has it upon retirement he was going to write a book, though no one was sure what kind of book the good Coroner had in him to write. "Got what I need for now," he said. "It is a crime scene, in case you had any doubts. I can tell you more about cause of death after I examine the remains. I'll be in contact. Nice to see you again, Ms. Rose." And, just like that, he walked off deep in analytical thought.

"How'd you get this one, Carl?"

He turned toward me as we started walking. "We got it fair and square."

Rolling my eyes at him, he continued before I could complain.

Using his fingers to tick off his mental list, he said, "There are some interesting coordination matters. Not 'jurisdiction'. Death occurred in Thurston County, til we know otherwise. There's the Feds with this park designation. The town of Littlerock is about to come into tourist season. We're sittin' on two county lines next to our own. We have Native American interests popping up. And, let's not forget the protected space activists around here in one group or another." He wiggled his fingers to emphasize his five points.

I noticed he didn't include the alien theory of the Mounds in any of those scenarios. I nodded in encouragement and couldn't help saying, "When this is over, remind me to tell you my theory on all this," I said pointing out and across the Mounds.

Dryly and not very convincingly, Carl looked at me without expression, "I can't wait."

Stepping through a maze of mounds, the Ranger popped into view.

"Holy shit," my screech echoed around me. "I thought you left," I added trying to recover.

Carl raised an eyebrow at the reference to shit being holy and all, good Christian that he is.

Ranger Dan smiled at my attempt to recompose. "I went to grab my stuff out of the truck." He lifted a bucket with, what looked like, gardening tools inside for us to see.

I put the Ranger under six feet tall, short by my standards. Topping out at five-six, my self-serving criteria may be due for an evaluation the next time I sit down with my new wine date, Francis Coppola's Claret.

We started walking again, one mound shadowing the next, and the next. A good time to get my first question out of the way. "The body was found this morning, right?" Of the few vehicles in the parking lot, I had seen only two County logos.

While they fumbled with who should answer, I made a choice. "Ranger Dan, how about you fill me in. You found the body, right?"

Carl stared at his notes, his way of observing people's behavior.

Dan took a deep breath and exhaled. The sun's rays bounced off the red hairs on his arms prickling as he recalled the vision and memory. "It was yesterday morning."

Resolving why so few officials and such limited activity were here now, I watched as the red sheen of the Ranger's hair rose with the sun climbing behind him. The vision played havoc with my eyes. I plunged into my bag after my sunglasses but came up short, remembering I'd opted for the light jacket instead. Aargh. Northwest marine weather.

Coming to an *'Army'* rest, he told his story. Upon his arrival at seven yesterday morning, he was surprised to see the local master gardener and his team of volunteers waiting at the gate. He learned they help with stewardship of the preserve every year by ripping out invasive plants. He opened the gate to the parking lot and the gardeners drove in and started disbursing themselves throughout the grounds. "I've walked sections of these fields over the past month just checking for downed branches and other debris from winter and spring storms. I never noticed this new mound," he reported to us, adding, "We're officially closed after Labor Day until Memorial Day weekend so there's not much activity here."

"What caught your eye?" Shading my eyes with my hand, I stepped to the side to keep from squinting at him.

"Well, the one mound was unlike the rest. The volunteer team made the discovery, called me over. Once I saw it up close, the difference pretty much stood out." He pointed to the area we were heading to and continued. "There's over six hundred acres here. As you can see, these mounds measure from fifteen to thirty feet across and up to eight feet tall. They number in the thousands and spread out from south of the Black Hills to Tenino." He went on to say visitors stroll along loop trails beginning with the upcoming Memorial Day weekend. His look over at Carl for confirmation brought nothing.

I was beginning to think these visitors might be spending their long weekend somewhere else this year, more than explaining the concerned look on Commissioner Whittier's face as she left.

We continued further into the Mounds. The Ranger continued our orientation to the Preserve. "The prairie changes with the seasons. Spring brings out blue Camas lilies. The golden grasses cover the grounds in the summer. Fall rains change the color scheme back to green. Pretty late spring this year and still cold," giving off a shiver as verification.

I waited for a description of the winter palette, but class was over for today. We were one mile into the two-mile trail when he stopped suddenly. I nearly plowed into him.

"And?" I wanted the full tour's worth.

He peeked back at me, squinting as he spoke, "Like all prairies, you'll find rounded stones like these." He stooped to pick up a couple of them in his newly gloved hand. He held them up for us to inspect. "The bottom two-thirds of this soil consists of glacial outwash, pale and full of pebbles. The top third consists of black silt earth. The soil of the one mound...," he paused in his narrative and then said, "Here, let me show you what I mean. Follow me."

He stood up quickly and, taking a hard left, he led us just off trail into a section close to a fence a quarter mile from a two lane County road. We pulled up in front of a mound; its appearance proving it was the product of inspection years ago.

Still wanting to feed my alien theory, "So, what was found inside this mound?"

He smiled his best Ranger smile. "Well, now, I wouldn't want to spoil the mystery, but I will tell you this. Mima prairie happened after glaciers retreated fifteen thousand years ago leaving this fast-drying gravelly soil behind. But," he added, "it doesn't really explain the Mounds," winking a blue eye at me. He knew a fellow conspiracy theorist when he saw one.

He and I bent down to inspect the previously dissected mound. The purpose of the bucket, gloves and tools became clear as he scooped up a small amount of dirt and put it inside a little jar, tightened the lid and labeled the jar, I pointed to the bottle. "What is that?"

"This," giving it a shake, "is one of the reasons the new mound is not like the rest. I'll show you. Let's go see."

He and I jumped back onto the paved section of trail, nearly knocking over Carl who had stayed put, observing from the designated path.

We followed the Ranger, crossing into the section where the remains were found. Approaching, the new mound was easy to spot now. Something or someone had been under all the dirt. I would have to rely on the pictures taken at the scene to see what had been discovered Friday morning.

Dan took a deep breath to steady his voice before speaking. Not making eyed contact with either of us, he stared at the ground. "As soon as I saw the thing up close, I could see it was newer than the others. I called my supervisor to report it." He looked up at us and said, "Of course, getting a response about a heap of dirt that don't look right didn't set off any alarms. My boss decided to call the Commissioner, 'cause she's close by. She came over. Decided she didn't like the looks of it, either. This *is* her back yard, after all," he reminded us. "That's when Detective Watson, here, got the call to bring an investigative team out."

Things were starting to make sense. Carl and his deputies would have been called to investigate a suspicious find, even if it turned out to be only a threat to the local tourism season.

The Ranger crouched down, under our watchful eyes, to scoop dirt from this now very much disturbed mound site. He put the sample in another little bottle and labeled it. He held up both. "As you can see, they're not the same."

I took both jars and looked at them closely. I had to agree. The second one contained what looked like any garden-variety dirt. Then it hit me. "Ahh. It wouldn't be until spring this mound would appear out of sync with the older ones."

Carl looked at me quizzically.

"Remember, there are seasons to the grasses and flowers that grow on these mounds. This new mound material would not have produced the same growth. It didn't have time to be seeded from the adjoining mounds growth. Weren't you paying attention, Carl?"

Ranger Dan's smile returned. "Right." Standing up and turning to go, "Gonna get these out of here." He held up the two little jars shaking them slightly.

"Hold on, Ranger. That dirt's not gonna go bad on us while we finish up here. Want you to stay around til my people show up. Then you're out of here for the day. This place is in lock down until I release it."

Nodding his understanding of his off duty status for the rest of the day, Dan stepped back from the yellow tapeline.

Carl took in the large expanse and then turned back to address the Ranger. "Aside from the road coming in here, are there other ways into this place?" He completed a half turn, using his arms to indicate he meant the whole preserve.

"Well, these are protected lands. Fencing all around." He thought on it, and then continued in his best Ranger voice. "I guess you could climb over the fence and walk through but not if you were bringing something in. Nah. The only way to get a body and dirt in here is down the main drive. We keep it locked during the off-season and at dusk during open season." He thought about what he said and added, "Or, you could take out a section of fence along one of those county roads and drive in. But, I haven't seen any damaged fence areas."

Running his hands through his dark brown wavy hair, Carl responded, "We don't know it was a body coming in or if it became a body once it got here."

Ranger Dan had a confused look on his face.

I saved him the trouble of asking. "He's saying the person might have been alive but was killed after he came here."

He nodded his understanding, then asked, "Do you know how long we're gonna be closed to the public, Detective? This is going to be hard on the budget if it's for very long."

"I'll do my best, Ranger. Earliest I can release it is after we have cause of death. Could mean us having to come back down and take another walk through, though." He left the rest unsaid.

Nodding, Dan went to await Carl's team. They would secure the area day and night until Carl released the site back to the Feds.

Coming up on noon, we piled into our separate vehicles. I grabbed my sandwich only to realize it was now inedible after hours in the car. The parking lot had warmed up and so had the mayo on my tuna and rye. Crap. Starting the engine, anxious to get myself to the nearest food source, I rolled down my window with a declaration. "We need to talk." Sounding less professional than I intended, I started to clarify.

Carl responded before I could. "How about after Church tomorrow. Lunch?"

"Ok. See you tomorrow, usual place?"

"Works for me."

CHAPTER 2

SUNDAY, MAY 22ND

I spotted Carl stirring his coffee at our regular table inside Hawk's Prairie Diner. I was looking forward to getting into details of the crime scene to help establish, in my own mind, the part I'd play in this investigation.

Carl stood up to greet me wearing his Sunday best, a yellow knit polo and khakis.

I dressed in my best denim jeans, white blouse, and a forest green fleece vest. It's not common knowledge, but fleece made its start in the Pacific Northwest. My story, anyway. I pride myself on being a principal investor in this all season fabric. Sitting together, we resembled a daffodil.

I sat down with a menu in hand and a "yes, please" to coffee. The server returned with a full coffee carafe, and we ordered.

Our working history together spans two years. During which time, I've had a variety of working titles. *'Investigations Consultant'* is the current. One title I insisted to Carl he not use is *'Profiler'*. I've spent too many years learning how *not* to assign labels to people to do a ninety-degree career turn. My education might have opened a door to a career profiling criminals as part of a day's work, but I closed that door, intentionally. Bluntly, I chose a profession allowing me to interact with people on a short-term, some might say 'shallow' basis. This is where both my skills and my shortcomings lie. But, to be perfectly frank, as long as the County could afford me as one of their civilian consultants, I'm on board under any hat.

I decided to ease into the case and not appear over eager for details. Instead, I inquired about his morning. "So, how was the sermon?" Big mistake.

"Darn Pastor preached on not using the Old Testament anymore. Wants to throw it out with the big flood."

I knew he was referring to Noah's day. I'm not a complete heathen. On hearing this, even I had to ask, "Why?"

"Says it's all about an angry, fed up God. Went on to say we should concentrate on the history of why we became Christians, the Good News the New Testament brought us. Wants us to focus on learning how to share the Love Jesus taught us and live by the code He left us." Carl ended with a slurp of his coffee. He checked quickly to see if he managed to spill any of it on his yellow shirt. He hadn't.

I find his struggle with the new Pastor, who's been with his Church for over a year, an interesting dynamic. Hoping the matter didn't end in fisticuff s in the sanctuary, I had to ask, "How'd it go over?"

"Depends on who you're asking."

"Okay, let's have *your* version."

"Well," I don't understand why he pulls this stuff on a perfectly good Sunday morning. Don't get me wrong. I generally like the man. He's done good work for us building our congregation. But, today he created more bad feelings than the entire Old Testament ever could. He raised the roof and not in a good way. When I left, he was telling the disgruntled masses he'd help get a study group together so's they could continue with the Old Testament. He, on the other hand, would be moving the congregation forward and preach only '*love*'. Geez. "

Our food arrived, providing topic relief. Missing lunch yesterday, I was hungrier than I thought. I added a side of fries to go with my salad and sandwich. The little voice in my head telling me I needed a break from counting calories and carbs. I hate watching my carb intake. It was all I did. Watch. And that just made me feel worse.

Carl diverted the conversation to my weak spot. He asked, "Speaking of *love-ins*, how's life in the commune?"

He was bating me. I bit anyway, "You know it's not a commune, Carl, it's a camping community."

Enjoying himself at my expense, he kept it going. "Yeah. What does that mean exactly, and what is it you like so much about that?"

Not letting him get the best of me, I quipped back, "Love of campfires. Why else." I often wondered about the appeal, myself. Living in a place where membership dictates hand waves to every passerby goes against my hermit nature and, mostly just rubs me the wrong way. And, the little gatherings meant to to solidify community make me run the other way.

Carl let it go for now. He looked up from his plate and said, "Stopped last night to pick up pictures from Ronnie. You know, the kid with the camera? I found an aerial shot on line of the whole area, taken a year ago, we can use. Printed it out at home. Not a bad rendition. Thought we'd head back to my Church after lunch and look this stuff over in more privacy." Then smirking, he continued with, "Can't think of an emptier place than a church building on a Sunday afternoon." He chuckled to himself.

I had to ask, being unfamiliar with protocol for use of a Church, "Is looking at pictures of dead bodies a proper use of the…."

He interrupted me with a sermon of his own, "We can use all the help we can get. Besides, Christianity had its start with the mystery of a dead body. Remember?"

I caught myself. No other comeback necessary.

We finished our meal and went to the front to pay our bill. He spouted out quick directions that turned out to be a location only a few miles from the restaurant. Told me to look for a sign with the words 'Christian Hope.' We'd meet at the front door.

He got into his personal vehicle, a Ford Excursion. We both

loved our Fords, or maybe we both just loved our Ford guy and mutual friend, Miles Craig. I once toyed with the idea of asking him out. It never came to be. I have a lot of those never came to be moments in my life.

I located the Church without any trouble. Carl pulled into the parking lot shortly after. My turn to throw a quick dig. "You could easily carry a body or three in that monster rig of yours."

He lifted out fresh lattes from our local Cutter's coffee house. It smelled wonderful. He watched as my eyes lit up and may have cracked a smile -- always hard to tell. Either way, I abruptly stopped talking. He won that round.

A revival tent look to the building, the double-glass doors featured an etching of Jesus standing with arms outstretched in a welcoming pose. I smiled recalling Carl's earlier story. Glancing back at my bright red car as he put the key in the lock, he rebounded with, "Not a good color choice for stakeouts."

Touché. "I don't do stakeouts in my line of work. It's frowned upon. Besides, I wouldn't talk if I were you. Royal blue metal flake doesn't exactly speak stealthy."

Both of us satisfied with the mutual barbs, we set the banter aside for now. He saw me looking at the set of keys he had pulled out of his pocket. "I have my own set. I'm the pianist for the praise band on Sundays," he responded before I could ask.

Two years and I don't know he's a musician? Geez. What I do know is his family is well to do. He grew up in Huntington Beach and both parents still lived in his childhood house. Let me think. Oh yeah, he's an only child. That's all I know about my crime-fighting partner's personal life. I should make more of an effort.

In a silly gesture of respect for my surroundings, I reached in my purse for a hair band tying it back from my face. I didn't want my hair getting in the way of looking over the photos, I told myself. I felt prim and proper now.

Carl pushed the doors open and Jesus appeared to step back allowing us to pass in front of him. Nice effect.

I followed him through the *'gathering place'*, the sign read. A poster sized photo of his newish Pastor caught my eye. I stopped and studied the wall hanging.

Carl turned to see what I was up to but said nothing.

The name on the plaque under the poster read *'Pastor Michael Gordon.'* He was wiry, tall, and had an athletic build. Handsome. In his fifties, I'd guess. Good eyes. Salt and pepper hair. Clean-shaven. And, good looking. Did I say that already? I wasn't going to guess his height, knowing my own tendency to miscalculate. He held some kind of banner. There were young student types with him. They all had their arms raised. The fingers on his left hand formed a peace sign; judging from the surrounds in the photo, I would summarize he was in a country appearing to not observe *'peace'* the same way we did, on more than one level. The Pastor sported a headband or maybe it was a sweatband. The young people around him seemed to be shouting something. I turned to ask Carl, but he had moved on.

A collection box asked for donations to help get a mission trip funded to Israel. In parenthesis underneath someone wrote, *'in two years when Pastor can legally re-enter the country'*. I dropped a dollar in for some spiritual insurance and caught up with Carl.

"Your Church is big on social action, then?"

"Social justice, yes." Carl made the distinction.

"What's the difference?" I tossed both words around, the distinction lost on me.

He didn't answer, opting to answer my unasked question. "Pastor, was booted out of Israel eight and a half years ago, during his last trip. Another year and a half, he can return without being arrested on the spot," shaking his head in annoyance as he finished the story.

I was certain *this* piece of the Pastor's background did not sit well with Chief Deputy Congregationalist, Carl Watson.

Carl opened a door to a good-sized meeting area with a large white quality composite table in the center and equally matched high quality chairs. The walls painted an easy on the eyes shade of white.

Expensive overhead skylights and recessed lighting accented the space. A nice environment for photo viewing. The taupe carpeting an expensive plush, the type you want to run your toes through, and dreamily find yourself heaven bound.

"Bet you wish you had this kind of lighting back at the office, huh?"

"I had a little something to say about the lighting in here, yes."

Clearly, Carl was still feeling the sting of his Sunday morning with the Pastor. Carl took pictures out of a manila envelope separating them into two stacks: *Before* the new mound and *after* the new mound. We began our study with the aerial photos dated April of last year. The black and white shot was a match to what we saw yesterday, Camas lilies in bloom, verifying this spring's vegetation to be one month behind schedule. We took turns using the magnifier glass he brought along and concluded that one year ago, no new mound. We had the year of death identified. It was a start. Dr. Bob would get us closer.

Carl said, "Authorized a crew to do a fly over tomorrow and see if we have more than one new mound or evidence of any other activity from when these photos were taken. Gonna widen our view to outside the immediate area about five miles into the farmlands. We should have those pictures by late afternoon." His team did an extensive walk through, he told me, but he wanted to be sure that nothing had been missed.

We continued combing through photos, pointing out to each other fences bordering the preserve, three farms, the entrance road, walking trails, restroom, small office, and a little spaceship shaped visitor kiosk. On second glance, maybe it was not a space ship. I'll go with a mound shaped kiosk.

We followed the curves along the paths in the photos and pinpointed the new mound location: seventy-five meters north of the large half moon curve and one mile into the two-mile loop trail. That would be a twenty or thirty minute one-way walk just to get from the parking lot to where the killer made his mound. We agreed it would be impossible for someone to bring in the victim and enough dirt without a key to the main gate or through some other entrance.

"Carl, out of all this acreage, why was this spot selected? What's so special about it? Was it simply a matter of time available?"

"Well, my theory from what I'm seeing in the photos is that many of the mounds in this prairie land are on private property. This spot may have been chosen for that reason; for privacy."

"Did you notice the new mound is smaller than others?"

"Could have been done deliberately done to hide it from view between the larger natural mounds."

I scanned over both sets of the photos again. "The new mound replaces a flat spot, but that's true of bunches of level areas throughout the Reserve field."

"I'm not seeing any other entrance other than the main gate."

We moved to the photos of the outlying areas. A few miles west, were hiking and horse trails, wetlands along Scatter Creek, and the Capitol State Forest. All of it popular for campers, hikers, hunters, and horseback, mountain bikes and motorcycle riders.

I stood up, stretching and pumping my arms finishing with a roll of my shoulders. Getting most of the kinks out from sitting hunched over, I said, "Access to the mounds from these forested areas we're looking at would go undetected, except for hauling dirt. Hauling in dirt meant using roads not trails."

Carl nodded without looking up.

I joined him back at the table. We shifted our view to the gravesite pictures. Looking closely at the undisturbed photos of the mound, the new one might have been written off as a prank or an intrusion into sacred lands. Soon, the new mound would be flattened out, or otherwise destroyed, removing the crime scene as part of the process, and forgotten.

The grave was not far below the top of the mound. Frame by frame, photo kid did a solid job cataloguing the extraction process. The photos exposing the body made my heart grow heavier with each picture. Mostly skeletal remains. Anything in close proximity, including some of the dirt and rocks, had been collected as evidence and sent off to the Morgue.

The killer *placed* the victim in this spot, I thought. No way had the body been just dumped here. Carefully laid out, dirt packed and mounded over him. He was lying on his back, arms at his sides. He appeared fully clothed.

"Carl, I think a lot of planning went into this. What do you think?" I did not see a spontaneous crime of passion; my little experience was telling me.

Carl shook his head, "Lot of questions on this one."

This was my first look at the full crime scene, where a life was taken. This could turn into a public relations nightmare fast.

Carl says he doesn't do press conferences. Wants to focus his attention in an undercover, behind the scenes, fashion. Says he learns more that way. Doesn't want the complications loss of anonymity would bring having his face plastered all over the investigation. I think his being a shy modest man has as much to do with it.

Now late afternoon, we stopped for the day. I left for home equipped with my own copies of the photos. I stopped for a fresh bottle of Black Label Claret, compliments of Francis Coppola and my neighborhood South Bay Grocer. Carl went back to witness the autopsy, chain of evidence and all. He and I would meet in his office at ten and wait for Dr. Bob's written findings.

*   *   *

Kicking off my Skechers, I let my bare feet warm up on the sun soaked deck. Blue sky, sun shining, and birds singing. Both the day and myself in balance with the universe. I changed into a short-sleeved Tee, choosing light pink to bring out the spring in my blue jeans.

Eyeing the bottle of wine, I said, "Hey, why not?" I uncorked it letting the wine breathe while I put dinner together. Finding

Foster Farm buffalo strips in the freezer, I settled on a dinner salad complete with baked buffalo chicken strips, chopped celery, romaine lettuce, and topped with blue cheese crumbles and dressing. You can never have too much cheese. First rule in my kitchen.

Although I carry extra pounds, I confessed it's the fault of the economy. Stress eating in tight times. Good save. I was ready for the wine. It was Sunday, after all.

Living alone, drinking red wine in the afternoon, and drinking by myself. Some might say I have issues. Who doesn't have issues? However, I argued, being single has many advantages. I only argue with myself, and I always win. Dinner is whenever I want it and in any fashion. And, I control the remote, twenty-four-seven. Living alone has its disadvantages too, but I try not to focus on those.

I scooped up my wine glass, glancing at the wall mirror. I can still turn a few heads, albeit older heads. Ash blonde hair, clear skin, and grey eyes reflected back at me. I took a second look, in case it needed a reminder.

Basking in the afternoon sun, I listened to a hoot owl make itself known. The blend of fir, white ash, cedar, pine, and crooked willow in this community landscape is *my* heaven. I take pride in having one of the few Garry Oaks here on my lot. The Garry is Washington's only native oak. The smell of a campfire and good-natured laughs a few lanes over, reminded me why I do live here. Camping. It leaves its own imprint, and it always brings a smile.

Not wanting to revisit the subject of living alone, I did have to wonder how having a housemate in a living space of four hundred square feet would work. I didn't see how anyone manages a relationship for very long. You'd have to be *really* compatible. Yet, out of two hundred memberships, over half consisted of couples. Albeit, most do not make this a permanent home. That had to be it.

Johnson Point Community began from a swath of reclaimed auctioned off farmland. Some old hippy made money off the tax rolls and had this idea to start an outdoor focused living community, modern day *'Walden Pond'* style.

Isolated living here is the norm in winter. Only half stick it out on these seventy acres. We have winter power outages, downed trees, and frozen water burst pipes in numbers like Dunkin' donuts has… well, donuts.

One of the things I like best is having no streetlights. I should remember that for the next time Carl asks me about my choice in living environments. When it's dark here, it's dark dark. Only a million stars lighting the way. The ten-foot wide main road, in contrast to the smaller side roads, allows the stars and moon to light the way. On the side roads, though, you're on your own.

I heard Leon rolling down the main road on his way to feed the fish in Huck Finn Pond. Leon is our land steward. He manages the great outdoors; his job is to insure we have healthy forests long into the future. He also ends up serving as hall monitor, security guard, and referee for those self-management challenged members. Leon and his crew also maintain our common facilities, which include showers, restrooms, clubhouse, party pavilion, and laundry buildings.

Another part of our common facilities Carl knows of firsthand. It's how I met him. The Club operates the only licensed camping club bar in Washington State, offering motivational drinking activities as if anyone here needs encouragement. The clubhouse includes the bar, a large open space, and a kitchen.

We have a kitchen service offering breakfast every Sunday morning and Friday night burgers and sandwiches. Good comfort food. Mid week, members throw potlucks and spontaneous food related events.

The smell of chicken wafting out from my oven onto the deck rang my dinner bell. While it cooled, I threw the rest together and made it back to the deck in time to enjoy the sounds of critters hurrying home for the evening. The trickling creek alongside my lot was frosting on the cake.

Soaking up all the natural benefits of this lifestyle, there was no doubt that the day was cooling off as the sun dipped below the evergreens. I grabbed my empty plate and wine glass and retreated inside.

Pouring another glass of wine, I corked the bottle and sat down at the keyboard, firing up my laptop. Two hours later, I had all the useful stuff I was going to be able to find for the night. Internet research is efficient but I find it very fatiguing. One thing leads to another and then another, and on and on, til you finally just have to pull the plug. I smiled recollecting a TV commercial along the same line. A woman is trying to talk to her friend, but every time she mentions any subject, she triggers an immediate regurgitation response from her friend who had spent far too long doing an internet search. Sensory overload. Me, too.

I spent a few minutes looking at the photos, then decided to put them aside, summarizing in my mind what I learned from them. The killer came into the Mounds at night through the entrance drive or through some other access area we had not yet discovered. Or, he or she came during the day in a vehicle raising no suspicion, perhaps affixed with a logo or official identification.

I look closer at the location of the new mound. The selected spot was out of immediate view of the bordering farms. So full moon, half moon, no moon, sun, or clouds, it wouldn't have mattered. Day or night. It was out of sight.

I flat out didn't want to think about this stuff anymore. I set my sights on pleasant dreams. Sunday night. 'Law and Order: Criminal Intent' re-run night. This is my longstanding Sunday night fix, time with Detective Bobby Goren's six-foot image before my eyes as I dozed off. A brilliant eccentric investigator, this man has this gift for gathering minor details, putting the smallest pieces of information together, and then working his way inside a murderer's head. Never mind his imposing and impressive physical presence..... Goodnight, Bobby.

CHAPTER 3

MONDAY, MAY 23RD

Thurston County government offices are located in downtown Olympia; a city with an eclectic array of hippy dining spots marking its heyday. The hippies have faded away, but the counter culture scene has not. Olympia is sprinkled with colorfully wrapped, loose fitting clothed people, some done up with dreadlocks. I have it on good authority Kurt Cobain used to live here in the early days of Nirvana. His grunge look is still alive, flannel shirts abound throughout the crowd.

Olympia has its seedy side, like every mid-sized city, evidenced by a dozen early morning transients sleeping along the sidewalks. A few dozen empty liquor containers and cigarette butts told the story of the previous night.

Tugging at my fleece vest, I walked through the parking lot making every attempt to look the part of the Olympia culture. My Birkenstocks didn't hurt the image. I stepped off the elevator at the third floor where most of the County's operations services, including public safety, are housed. The Commissioners' offices and the legal beagles occupy the fifth floor. I think the fourth floor houses the financial types. Doc and his team have the first floor, which doubles as the basement. I'm not sure what's on the second floor. I've never looked.

I think my promptness is something Carl appreciates about me. Not like I ever asked. But, his nod and half smile as I entered gave me confirmation it was in his top ten. He stood up pointing to a small conference table. We both took a chair.

"Good morning. How you doin' so far?" He folded his hands in front of him on the table awaiting my response.

No point in avoiding it; he wasn't going to say another word until he was satisfied with my response. "Just fine," I answered in my most casual nonchalant voice.

His question addressed my uneasiness in dealing with the family dynamics aspect in our murder cases. They all have them in one way or another. Family relationships are not my specialty. I keep those types of mediation cases out of my practice.

Who am I kidding? I'm all relationships challenged. I bestowed my uneasiness a name to give it more credibility. I call it LAD or Loss Affect Disorder. A condition centered on an inability to grow close to people for fear of losing the relationship.

I decided to nip Carl's concern in the bud. "There's no family stuff in this thing yet, Carl." As an afterthought, I added, "You know, just because I have no family, doesn't mean I'm allergic or something."

Now peering at me over a document, he lectured, "You really should have that looked at."

I didn't reply. He made it sound like some kind of rash, which it isn't. I just steer clear of getting mixed up in other people's family dysfunction. A choice I made, that's all. I reinforce that choice by not specializing in divorce mediations, especially. That counts for treatment, does it not? Or at least disorder management. Carl would probably call it *'self medicating'*. I changed the subject. "Any belongings found with the victim?"

"Nope. No wallet. No watch. No rings. Nothing but the clothes on his back and the shoes on his feet." Giving me an *oo-we-oo voice, he added,* "No apparent murder weapon found."

"Apparent?" He may have guessed my mound's theory after all.

"No gun. No knife. Nothing found in the immediate area. Got a lot of rocks and pieces of wood. Nature's weapons. Plenty of those." He looked up from the papers he was thumbing through and said, "Until I have cause of death, we won't be searching the brush, though. I'll keep a team posted until we know where the murder occurred. Doc's testing the soil for blood residue."

"What are you reading?"

"Preliminary autopsy and lab reports," he held them up.

"Already? That's good news."

"Not good news. No prints. No blood or DNA. No defensive wounds. Nothing off the clothing. Too deteriorated from the muddy winter. Nothing in the grave site but the remains." Looking up he gave me a little wink and added, "No ritualistic items found for any of your mounds theories, in case you're wondering."

Moving on and off that subject, "Do we know where the dirt came from?"

"No. Very labor intensive. I'm putting it on hold for now."

"How about cause or time of death? And, identity of the victim?" I was anxious for details.

His eyes lit up a bit. "Hey, slow down. We're here all morning, and you came in, what, all of half an hour?"

I took a deep breath to curb my enthusiasm. I fiddled with the zipper on my vest. Then decided to take it off and set it in the chair next to me.

"From the condition of the remains, Bob puts time of death in November or December. One of my guys is going through missing persons reports."

"One more reason to hate our rainy winters. Shoe or vehicle tracks are history, right?"

He looked up from his reading. "Ain't that the truth? *Cal-i-for-nye-ay* this ain't. Remains put his age in his late 20s, early 30s. Athletic frame. Maybe worked out or worked outside. No identity yet."

Carl kept reading, but not aloud.

So, I asked, "Do we have a cause of death or identification of the murder weapon?"

"Doc's taking a closer look, and preparing the final report. He'll come up here once he's done." He flipped through another page. "No gunshot or knife wounds. Doesn't think its strangulation, but isn't ready to rule it out just yet."

He looked up toward the ceiling, thinking, then back at me. "It's a stretch, but we don't know it wasn't a pauper burial."

"A what?"

"Buried by family to save on funeral costs."

And he wonders about my family relationship issues.

"You don't really think that, do you?"

"No. Wouldn't be conducive to visiting the gravesite without risk of being caught. Our victim was young; he'd have family and friends in his life. Naw, I'm gonna go out on a limb and rule that out."

"Okay, that's a start. Ruling something out, that is."

Carl let me know he, too, was anxious to have something to work with. "Doc's making this case a priority. Everyone and everything cranked open to full speed."

Doing the math, dead five to six months ago, I made a hesitant prediction of my own. The resolution trail may already be colder than a Northwest spring.

Doc will give it top priority. Somebody's son is dead. The rush priority might also have something to do with the amount of County money being spent keeping the Reserve guarded until it can be released back to the Park. I was certain the bean counters were dotting every *i*' and crossing every 't' to come up with ways to bill the Feds every which way they could. Still, 'round the clock security couldn't last too much longer, tourist season is rapidly approaching.

At half past eleven, the phone rang. Carl grew preoccupied with a string of incoming and outgoing calls.

I let my mind wonder to Doc's impressive quarters with its autopsy tables and instruments. His digs include top of the line X-ray, photo processing and magnifying equipment, computerized surface magnification and photographic equipment, and a newly acquired Histology Lab. With so many cuts in the County budget, the Medical Examiner's office hadn't been subjected to any. I guess twenty years as County Coroner gets you all kinds of budget protection.

Once Doc establishes cause and time of death, suspicious deaths are kicked upstairs. The County Sheriff, Carl's boss, takes charge of the case. The death becomes a formal investigation, including notifying friends and relatives. Carl's team handles hostage situations, sniper incidents, bomb threats, hazmat explosions, viral agent threats, civil unrest, mass arrests, terrorism, and any death that gets bumped up to murder.

Thinking back to when I first joined Carl's team, it was after he returned from a visit to his parents' home over some holiday, can't remember which one.

He corralled them into answering questions about his early childhood. They confirmed what he concluded by researching on his own. They confessed that they had kept test results to themselves and off record not wanting their son to grow up with any attached stigmas. Carl's condition, he told me, had a name, "*high functioning Asperger's Syndrome.*" Being a mental health professional of sorts, I knew something about the social style, or lack of, associated with the condition.

In Carl's case, turning whatever limitations there may have been into a successful career, his obsessive single-minded focus and limited facial expressions were just what the doctor ordered for detective work.

Coincidentally, when he returned home, he landed a call out to the Johnson Point Community Bar. The incident involved two of our members playing dueling golf carts, a popular mode of transportation here. Not the dueling part. Clearly, they were toasted. Technically, they weren't driving drunk as they were in a private club parking lot. He made a lot of noise about dragging their butts off to jail, which put the two into instant best friend mode; all forgotten, until the next time these two went after each other. They are one of several Community sore spots. Not the image we want to portray in our sales brochure. After he had diffused the situation, he sat me down to go over the incident. He started to lecture me about over serving alcohol. As the on duty volunteer bartender, I let him know those two arrived in their present condition, I hadn't served them anything.

We started talking and sharing background information. His vacation and discovery came into the conversation. It was weighing fresh on his mind. He was feeling vulnerable, questioning his ability to do his job now that he knew what he knew. Wondering if he should report it. Through talking it out, he came to a place of peace and resolved to work harder to be the best officer he could be.

People tell perfect strangers things they would never tell their closest friends. We've all done it.

I shared my career and work experience, throwing in a family secret of my own so we were on the same level of trust with each other.

He decided he needed my kind of touchy-feely', his words, expertise available at times during his casework. He sold it to his superiors the next day.

The silence in the room brought me back from reminiscing. Carl had finished his calls and sat waiting for me to return. I blushed. "Any news?"

Carl looked back at his notes before answering. "We got an ID from the victim's dental records. He had some extensive work done recently which helped." He looked up. "Are you ready?"

"I am. Let's have it."

Leaping up, Carl moved to his white board, his case-diagramming tool of choice. He chose his blue dry marker. "His name is Jacob Mathews; went by Jake. Twenty-six years old. Just under six feet tall. He's an only child. Weighed a hundred eighty pounds when last checked. Did a four-year stint in the Army. Lived with his dad since he was discharged from the service. I have a copy of his military

ID and records coming from Fort Lewis-McChord. And, DMV is sending over a copy of his WA State driver's license."

"If you're getting a photo of him, why do you need his other ID.? Nobody looks like their driver's license picture, by the way." Thank God, I thought to myself. "Now that we know his identity, how much use is it?"

"No stone unturned."

Thinking it through, it made sense. No ID was found on Jake's body. Looking at what should have been there might tell us why it was taken.

"Received next of kin information from the base commander. That led us to his father. He lives in Tacoma. We'll talk to him more about the rest of the family once we meet with him. I want you involved in the interview. You okay with that?"

"Of course." I wondered how quickly I could come down with a twenty-four hour bug.

Carl cleared his throat and continued. "No information on the name of the outfit where Jake worked, other than it was in construction. He's been out of the Army about a year. Mrs. Mathews died a few years back. He and his son didn't spend as much time as they used to since she passed. He's bringing recent photos and everything else he has that might help us know his son better.

"Single?" I asked.

"Mr. Mathews says Jake had a girlfriend. He has a picture of her he's bringing with him. He was trying to recall her name. We can use the photo of her to try to get an ID."

"How about close friends?"

"One for sure, Paul Dobson. Told him to bring names and numbers of any of Jake's buddies he could remember." Finished with the white board, Carl put the marker down and went back to his desk. He picked up a sheet of paper and looked up. "I thought we'd find a lead from his bank."

"How's that?"

"Paper trail of his recent activities. Unfortunately, for us, Jake was a cash guy. Didn't use credit cards or debit cards. Deposited his paycheck and immediately withdrew most of it til the next deposit. No trail that help with his last known whereabouts.

"Doesn't that seem a bit odd in today's cashless world?"

"It does. Not sure what it means, but it's worth looking into further. I'll put someone on obtaining a copy of all deposit and withdrawal records."

I decided now was the time to share my thoughts on access to the Mounds that I'd been working over in my head. "I've been thinking about how the killer got into the Mounds."

Carl looked up and said, "And?"

"The only way to get into the Mounds is if the killer had official reason to be in the preserve, had a key to the gate to the parking area, or knew of another entrance." As I let him digest that rather obvious conclusion, it hit me. "Carl, he had to have a large vehicle, a truck, to bring in enough dirt to build his mound. And, I know why he chose the spot."

Carl said, "Go on, You have my attention."

"It's the one of the few places out of view of the farms across from the preserve." I spread out the pictures I brought from home.

Carl moved away from his desk and walked to the table, studied them, and nodded his agreement saying, "Nice job, Lynz."

"Something I've been wondering is about the Commissioner's hands-on involvement at the crime scene."

"Those old theories the Mounds are sacred Indian burial sites. The Commissioner's immediate concern was to avoid the entire field being at risk to scavengers looking for artifacts. She went off to a meeting to put out that fire. Now, with the fact our victim is not a Native American, she'll have even more good news to share regarding the sanctity of the Preserve." He moved around his office stretching, then, "From the position of the body and lack of any sacred items, we were ninety percent sure yesterday. Being able to say the victim is a white Caucasian in our public statement should keep all potential treasurer hunters away."

"So, it narrows it down to just your run-of-the-mill white guy, then?"

Carl didn't respond but looked at me curiously.

Slightly embarrassed at my own politically incorrect charged comment, I changed the subject and asked, "When do you take the case public?"

"Once we get the official report from Doc with all the particulars, I'll take it to the Sheriff. He'll take it to the PR folks who'll put the spin on it they decide best works for our case and meets our obligation to keep the public informed."

As if waiting for his cue, the Coroner stepped off the elevator reading as he walked. He came through the door, without missing a beat, sat down and launched into his report. "We have manner of death. Suffocation brought on by being buried alive. I found a mysterious puncture wound on the back of his neck. Made by a small pointed instrument, an ice pick, perhaps. From the state of the remains, I can confirm my original statement that our young man died late November to mid December, which is enough time to decompose to the skeletal and tissue remains to the condition we have downstairs."

He looked up expectantly at both of us. Not hearing us ask the question, He proceeded as though we had. "Many variables interfere with decomposition, including environment and soil acidity. A body buried six feet deep in ordinary soil, for example, can take ten to twelve years. Immerse the body in water, and decomp speeds up considerably. Exposed to air, it occurs eight times faster. The skeleton itself is not permanent either; acids in soils can reduce it to unrecognizable components....."

Carl raised his hand to stop the Doctor's rambling. "Bob. Was he murdered?"

Doc went back to his report, flipping through several pages before answering. "Oh yes, of course. It's right on this page here. I flagged it for you. Consistent with our preliminary findings. You already know his identity." Doc scanned through the rest of his notes. "I found no blood at the burial mound. If he was killed in the paved parking area and then brought to the site, the winter rains long washed away any evidence."

Satisfied with what he'd heard so far, Carl steered the Doctor back to cause of death. "You say a small puncture wound. Like an ice pick? Show me exactly where the wound was made and the kind of damage it caused."

Doc jumped up and crossed the room. "Yes, well, another interesting discovery, the insertion point." He clipped the x-ray to the view box installed in Carl's office, bringing us to our feet and over next to him as he did.

We peered at the screen while he pointed to the small wound near the base of the skull. It was easy for me to see, once he pointed out the tiny spot on the film.

I asked, "Doc, would that kill him? I see from your report he was in good shape, a tall healthy young man."

"All very true." he answered. "The wound is to the spinal cord. Damage at the third cervical vertebra. Without immediate attention, an injury of this sort would certainly bring about death or, at best, the patient would require a respirator to live. Our killer may be someone with medical training, or someone else who would know the paralyzing damage this wound would cause."

Doc thought more about it, then looking directly into Carl's eyes, he said, "This was no lucky hit. Our killer had to have some specialized knowledge or medical training."

"If not medical training, perhaps someone with specialized military training," Carl thought aloud.

Doc stroked his chin then nodded at Carl's suggestion.

I came back to the victim's seemingly obvious advantages over an attacker. "How did a kid in good shape, with Army training himself, get into a position for an injury like this to be inflicted?"

"Yes, Ms. Rose. It troubles me as well." Doc looked stumped.

"It could be as simple as he trusted the person or persons he was with," Carl volunteered.

Doc raised two fingers to indicate he had something else. He said, "Whether or not he knew his attacker, I have a third discovery that might, and let me emphasize 'might' help us understand how it happened. There were traces of ground ivy in his teeth."

Both Carl and I jerked our heads around with the same puzzled look on our faces.

Doc extended his two fingers to a full stop to head off our question. "It's possible it was used to subdue our victim. The plant is very bitter on its own. Not something you'd consume accidentally. Had to be in something he ate. Of course, there's no way to know what that was from the remains. The stomach is long gone. What I do know about ground ivy has to do with its affect on horses. I don't want to say anything more right now. I'll have more for you when I can confirm my hunch on its potential affect on humans."

Carl's voice rose slightly in frustration, "Doc. Was he poisoned, paralyzed or suffocated?"

"Oh, sorry. Let me be clearer. The puncture wound would have paralyzed him. Suffocation *was* the immediate cause of death."

"Oh, no. Don't tell me," I started.

Doc confirmed my worst fear. "Yes, my second discovery. I'm sorry to say, Ms. Rose, what little breath he had left, he took through dirt. We found enough lodged in his throat area to draw our conclusion he was alive when he was buried."

I shivered at the image of breathing through dirt.

Carl thanked Doc and dismissively picked up his phone to call his Deputies on duty at the Preserve. "Time of death is November to December."

Doc took his cue and left.

Carl continued listening and responding in turn, "Cause of death is suffocation. Puncture wound to the back of the neck brought about enough paralysis to keep him from fighting back. Comb the area for a possible weapon, small ice pick sized. Once you're sure we didn't miss anything, release the area back to the Ranger. Leave the area taped off in case we need to revisit..." He ended the call and stood up to see me looking at him.

"I'm thinking, since you don't refer to the Ranger by name, he's on your suspect list?"

"Let's just say he's a person of interest. He meets my criteria."

I scanned the Coroner's report. I'm a little curious myself, after reading Doc's report, why the Ranger took those dirt samples. The Doc's notes say he took his own."

"Now that's worth asking him about." He made another note to the case file. "We'll set up interviews with the Ranger, his friend Paul, and the victim's girlfriend. You'll need to keep your calendar open this week. This is when I need you doing your thing."

He meant my experience at drawing people out, repositioning them from their defensive postures. It's what makes mediation successful.

Next on Carl's list of things to do included briefing his boss, the County Sheriff, who would then brief the Commissioner. The public relations staff would fine-tune a script for a public statement.

The Commissioner's to-do list, Carl told me, would include a meeting with the Council of the Nisqually Nation to give assurance the crime was not about disrespecting Native American people.

"Lynzee, we'll meet for coffee in the morning. Then take a drive down to Littlerock before the looky-loos get down there. Talk to some of the farmers and townsfolk. Find out what they remember about the holidays last year." Carl watched as I processed the plan.

"Okay. I don't know how much detail we can expect people to remember, though. I don't think I could recount much of my own November and December if I had to." I nodded waving goodbye as he dialed the phone. I closed the door behind to Carl setting the stage for tomorrow's press conference.

"Sheriff, glad I caught you. I have some news and a request...."

*   *   *

I stopped to take care of errands I had planned for the rest of the week. Once home, I made a dash outside to my ten by twelve cabin that sat at the far side of my lot. I needed a little R & R. I call the space my *'family room'. It has a* workbench, stool, shelving unit, and a futon. I'd recently moved in a small piano. To complete the room, I hung sheets of pegboard on all four walls, covering seams and lining window casings in bright white trim. The pegboard allows me to move memory pieces from hook to hook and not leave holes behind. I change the memorabilia period a few times a year to reinforce family memories from different decades.

'Family', I thought. It can bring out the worst in people. When mom and dad died five years ago, we'd not spoken for years. Our estrangement started years before that as we continually found excuses to remain cutoff from each other. Prideful excuses. My twin found herself caught up in the middle of this battle of wills and wouldn't risk her relationship with her parents for one with her sister. So, she had no contact with me when they didn't. She needed them more than she needed a relationship with me. I told her I understood. I didn't.

When she died in a horrific car crash three months after mom's death, I held my breath for another three months, then a year, crossing my fingers and hoping I wasn't next. But, as friends tried to tell me, God still had something else planned for me.

Family took on a new purpose after her death, something I experienced by myself in a manageable way. Family turned into *'place'* and *'things'*, not *'people'*.

Pushing those memories aside, I started polishing and scrubbing old hand tools once belonging to my dad. I removed the rust off his wood saws then fed the handles with an oil-based stain. I grew up hearing the sounds of these very saws working their magic, marveling how these little acts stirred up such pleasant recollections. Dad working in the garage with his sawhorses stretched out and his carpenter pencil tucked behind his ear. He built our house in the small town of Ruston, in the North end of Pierce County, out of a salvaged abandoned building. It had once been a smelting ASARCO company employees' clubhouse. The building was rumored to have carried its own history and secrets.

I picked up his levels. Old wood in need of nurture and care. I used to watch him line up the tiny bubbles before he moved to the next part of his project. Restoring all his tools into pristine shape was akin to bringing him back to life, or, maybe, bringing me back to life. No doubt about it.

Last year, I restored the only picture of dad's fishing boat. An oil painting. A stranger presented it to him when I was just a kid. It hung in our living room til the day he died. The artist had watched my dad netting bait and unload into special holding pens at Pt. Defiance Boat House. He had captured the moment on canvas. I'm glad he did. There are no photos in existence.

Years of sloppy storage left its mark on the canvas. I didn't know a thing about painting anything other than a wall or my toenails. Still, I worked tediously on matching colors at a local art store, then applying careful brush strokes until all the stains of time were gone. Colors blending perfectly, surprising me. Back to how it looked when I was growing up.

Dad and one of his five brothers were commercial fishermen, business partners. They each had their own boat and always fished together. They made a good living once upon a time. Right up until Judge Boldt's historic ruling involving the fishing rights of Washington's Indian Tribes over non-Indian people. His decision enraged non-Indian commercial fishermen. Fishermen just like my dad and his brother. Bitterness replaced cash flow in dad's life. Bitterness accumulated in his life and showed on his face right up to the day Judge Boldt left this earth.

Dad's many prejudices were a big dynamic in why he and I didn't see eye to eye. Once I was old enough to know he was wrong, like all teenagers, I let him know. He believed differences made enemies. He didn't appreciate my opposing viewpoint, no matter how many times I tried to force it on him.

The sudden sounds of birds and critters scurrying about outside on their way to their nests and families snapped me back into the present. I smiled and took a deep breath, exhaling as I looked around. I closed the door behind me with a, "Goodnight family."

Back inside, I sliced Asiago cheese bread to go with Rotini chicken noodle soup, ala Progresso. I reflected back on Carl's reference to me *'doing my thing'* and why I chose mediation over a counseling career.

I traced my career choice to the memory of my dad's twenty-year feud with our neighbor over a fence. As any decent mediator will tell you, it wasn't about the fence. The matter went much deeper, twenty years deeper. Many years later, I tried to convince him to meet with a mediator. He wanted a lawyer. I brought him one, but dad would hear nothing about mediation from him either. In the end, it caused yet another rift between us. The only new information I got out of the whole ordeal was learning the matter stemmed from some insult to mom and the demand for an apology, which the neighbor was finally willing to make to put an end to it. Dad said no to the apology, it was too late, he said. He chose to take his anger, an all too familiar part of his life, to his grave.

The inspiration to become a mediator came from an entirely different source. A favorite storybook I read growing up called *'Once Upon a Time in Storyland'*. One of the stories featured King Solomon's visit from the Queen of Egypt and her attempt to fool him with two floral bouquets of roses and lilies. She spent a fortune having one bouquet designed to look and smell like the real deal. The other bouquet, identical in every detail, contained the genuine flowers. She held them at a short distance in front of the King. She asked him to identify the real bouquet. She told him he was not permitted to touch either one nor move any closer to them. She moved to stand a few feet away from where he sat on his thrown. Plenty of onlookers lined the hallways in the palace, familiar with their King's skill and wisdom. They eagerly awaited another illustration. King Solomon studied the bouquets and prayed for guidance. In the tranquility of his prayer, he heard a tapping sound apparently unheard by others in the palace. Looking around, he caught sight of a single bumblebee buzzing against a window. He motioned to a guard to open the window. The bee flew in, still without notice by anyone else. It flew directly into the true flowers held by the Queen, ignoring the false bouquet she held in her other hand. The King chose his bouquet utilizing all of the gifts God bestowed on him to solve a problem. That sold me. I was hooked. The gift part, anyway.

Hot soup. Toasted bread. I made quick work of my dinner. Once finished with the cleaning up portion of dining, I turned off the electrical switch to the water heater. It saved bunches on my utility bill to do this, and I was glad I had it installed. Heat what's needed, when needed. Then turn it off. Environmental stewardship is part of the eclectic community environment we share here.

I was ready to call it a night and channel surfed until landing on a rerun of 'Criminal Intent'. Perfect. I wondered if I watched these reruns often enough, I could learn how to capture the moment in a case the way Detective Goren does. The moment when the crime unravels. The moment when the truth is known. The moment when, without a word and evidenced through a slight bow, he clasps his hands behind his back, tips his head to one side, and offers that half smile into the face of the accused that can only mean, "Gottcha."

Well done, Bobby.

CHAPTER 4

TUESDAY, MAY 24TH

Carl sat at our usual table. I plopped down with a question. "Coffee or Breakfast?"

He suggested we order breakfast and plan for a long day, and we did. It arrived shortly after.

"We have a change in plans. Our Littlerock Commissioner wants us to interview Ranger Dan on site. The Ranger's supervisor complained he's got too much to do in preparation for opening day for him to drive back and forth to Olympia. Sheriff's backing her up."

"I thought the place was opening Friday, the start of Memorial Day Weekend." A political decision by the name of opportunity must be lurking in the shadows.

"Commissioner recommended an earlier opening date to put the incident behind us. Thinks it's in everybody's best interest to release the Preserve back to the Feds. Sheriff agrees. There's some sort of ' hush-hush' co-operative land exchange deal in the works between the County and Feds. The County hopes to operate the place as a moneymaker. In exchange, the Feds want to trade for a piece of property above my pay grade to know much about."

I nodded giving him a 'mum's the word' zip across my lips.

"The press conference is this morning. Expect people to head down the minute news of the body found in the Mounds hits the airwaves. Press, too. So, opening day is tomorrow."

"No reason to protect the crime scene anymore?"

"I argued we should keep access restricted until we catch the killer, but the cost benefit analysis didn't play out for the Sheriff. I couldn't offer much to change his mind. The murderer brought in dirt and didn't disturb nearby mounds. The scene is nearly six months old. We've no evidence to suggest the crime even took place where we found him. If I held those cards in a poker game, I'd fold."

"It doesn't sound like much when you put it like that."

He summed it up with, "Our Ranger's gotta lot of dirt to move out. All the stakeholders agree there's no place for it there. Has to come out."

"We have today before the onslaught, then?"

He put his fork down feeling for his napkin, "Yep. This is the shot we have before things get crazy with news and crime junkies."

I hurried through my last bight of Eggs Benedict and asked, "Do we leave from here?"

"We do. Ready? You can ride with me. We'll leave your vehicle in the parking lot. It will be safe. Unless you want me to follow you back to the Commune......"

I stopped him. "No, no. Let's just leave from here and save time."

We started for the door when his cell rang. He answered and nodded a lot then signed off. "That was Ronnie. The new aerial photos didn't show any disturbances at the Mounds he could pick out. I'll go over them tomorrow and let you know if I see anything we haven't already factored in."

"Ronnie? The intern photographer I met the other day?"

"Yeah, he was thrilled as a new father for the opportunity to do an official shoot from our helicopter. Gonna put it on his resume. Saved us money, too, him doing the developing himself."

We paid up and reached the County white and green sedan. "I'm not going to ride with you if I have to sit in the back, Carl."

He opened the passenger door, bending at the waist while ushering me toward the front seat with a sweep of his arm. "I wouldn't have it any other way," a hint of amusement in his voice.

During our half hour drive to Littlerock, I reviewed signs to watch for during our upcoming interviews: Variation in pitch or pace of speech. A surge in the use of 'ums' and 'ahs.' Breaks in eye contact. Body shifting away from a question. Covering face or mouth when speaking. Licking of lips. Nervous tapping of fingers or feet. Yep, just like riding a bike.

Turning off the engine, Carl said, "This will be quick."

I looked up from my thoughts to find we'd arrived in Littlerock. The sign said the town was named after a rock in the original postmaster's yard. Keeping things simple out West. The smallest of small communities, the town included a gas station, a grocery store, a church, hardware store, and an all grades school.

"No shit," I thought, hoping not aloud.

Carl seemed un-phased in either case. We got out of the car.

I stretched to help shift breakfast down past the waistband of my beige cargo pants. Carl ate fruit with his meal. He didn't need to perform this same maneuver or the one where I pulled the bottom of my cotton knit shirt to make it longer.

The air smelled of fresh cut grass, hay, dairy cows, and newly turned dirt.

"I'm gonna talk to the gas station and store folks," he told me. You, wander around inside the stores. Check for anything small and sharp enough for a murder weapon." He walked toward the owner who was coming out wiping his hands on a cleanup rag.

I walked into the gas station store but came up empty. Next stop, the market. No ice picks for sale here. A corkscrew caught my eye. I bought the thing, just in case it fit the description of the wound we saw in Doc's X-rays. If it didn't, I wouldn't let it go to waste. Carl talked to the storeowner.

On the way back to the car, I spotted an area off to the right with, amazingly enough, dirt for sale and a handy little front loader parked nearby.

Carl walked up next to me, thinking what I was thinking. "We'll take a sample of this. Pretty handy location so close to the murder site. I'll go back in and find out who's in charge of selling dirt."

"Anything from the station owner?"

"Doesn't remember unusual activity or any strangers around last winter. Both admit to a lot of holiday preparations, and parties. Business was secondary to celebration."

"I bought a corkscrew."

He gave me a sideways look.

"It was the only thing remotely like the description of the murder weapon," I explained.

He looked at it and then at me. "I'll be right back," he said disbelievingly.

As we started toward the Mounds, Carl shared what he learned about the dirt. "Soil sales go with the store. I asked for copies of records of any truckload sales in November or December. He's going to check and get back to me. Didn't remember any. By then, he told me, planting season is pretty much over. Said he'll check his September and October records, too."

"That make him curious?"

"He started to ask, but I brushed off my shield here," pointing to the badge on his shirt, "and he opted to not inquire."

"Wow, you played your power card. You didn't resort to drawing your gun on him, too, did you?"

"What? There really was a speck on it."

"Yeah, right."

"You have plans for your corkscrew?"

"Hey. I was serious. It is the only thing I found in either store that might fit the entry wound description. I wasn't going to come back completely empty handed."

"Okay. I'll give it to Doc. If it's not a match, you'll get it back. You can put it to other uses."

I didn't respond.

We drove along the County road on our way to talk to the neighbors facing the Mounds on the off chance they remembered unusual lights or activity last winter.

The first stop had a young family with too many kids running around, for my taste. An adult female told us they'd only moved in a few months ago. We moved on. The farm in the middle was next.

This neighbor looked anxious to talk to us. He walked toward us from the barn as we came to a stop in the gravel drive. "Hello folks. Name's Ralph. Ralph Connors." He held out his hand in greeting as he approached us.

We got out of the car and shook hands with the epitome of a picture perfect American farmer, generations of farmers embedded in the lines on his face. Overalls, red paisley handkerchief, rubber boots, and chewing on a blade of prairie grass. It didn't take long to conclude he was mostly lonely and would have greeted a bill collector with the same enthusiasm.

Carl introduced himself. I did the same; then asked if he was all alone.

"Yep. Just me. Lot of work since my wife died some years back." He did a sweep with his arms to indicate a good-sized farm once upon a time.

I shut down the self-pity party forming in my thoughts. "I'm sorry. Goodness. How do you keep this place going?" I was genuinely curious.

"I'll tell ya. It gets harder every year."

I made his age around seventy.

Carl was making the same calculations. Sir. . ." he started.

"Just call me Ralph." He ushered us to a picnic table in front of his whitewashed farmhouse, complete with a white picket fence. The American dream he now lived out alone. "Just everyday folks down here."

"Ralph, what all do you raise here on the farm?"

He smiled at my choice of words, rubbing the sweat from his brow, adjusting his straw hat in the process. The day was warming up. I figured just moving around for Ralph was exhausting enough, having nothing to do with the weather.

"Well, just finished feeding the chickens and pigs. I sell the pigs for slaughter. Chickens and eggs are for me. I've been selling off sections in two acre parcels as the County allows out here. I hire help when I need to."

No way would this sweet old guy be killer, I thought, but the questions were still going to be asked.

"You do any planting or grow any crops?"

"Used to. My son moved away, farm life wasn't for him. I plant a few flowers every spring in remembrance. We used to take my wife's geraniums to the County fair every year. Won most years, too."

Carl broached the first topic. "You haul in dirt or use what's here?"

"We got good soil on this farm. No need to bring it in," he challenged.

Carl went in another direction. "You hear anything about some goings on at the Mounds?"

"Well, now that you mention it. Did hear a few things. That why you here talking to me?"

"The story will come out in the next few days. We found a body. Seems it's been there all winter." I took note Carl excluded the part about the body being buried.

"Well, don't that just put Littlerock on the map now? We'll have all kinds of folks out snoopin' around soon, I reckon."

"You notice any unusual activity? Say November or December, last year?"

I watched Ralph wince a little. I asked if he was okay. "I'm fine. Just miss my wife so much every Thanksgiving and Christmas, you know? Holidays are the worst."

I wasn't going anywhere near that. Carl pushed on.

"It's dark pretty early those months. Perhaps headlights or flashlights out in the Mounds where they shouldn't be?"

"Can't recall anything." Still pondering he added, "Pretty mild season as I remember it, weather wise. Spent a lot of time in town helping with tree sales. Picked up a little extra cash." He drifted off in his own thoughts and memories.

I was starting down holiday lane, too. I changed the subject. "Ralph, do you know who owns the place next door to you?" I pointed at the farm to the left of his.

"Oh, you won't find anybody. Place was auctioned off last fall. Some bank owns it. Hey, it was right around November if that helps?"

"Just might. Thanks for bringing it to our attention. We'll check County records and see what we can find out."

Ralph asked us to stay for some lemonade. We declined, saying we were on County time and thought it best we move along. Carl gave Ralph his personal line business card and told him to call if he remembered anything. He nodded in appreciation of our being responsible public service employees. There are county time-clock people all over Thurston County when it comes to taxpayer dollar accountability.

We got into the car. Carl started the engine. "Next stop. Our Park Ranger."

I'd been quiet during our interview with Ralph but now I asked Carl, "Should we have asked for a tour of the barn? Check to see if anything might fit the description of the murder weapon?"

"I didn't want him spreading any information about what kind of weapon we're looking for just yet. News spreads like a prairie grass fire in these small towns."

"Clever. I'm glad I didn't blow it for you."

"I should have mentioned my approach for the day earlier. The call from Ronnie got me off track."

"It all worked out. So, fill me in now."

"The press packet will include a picture of Jake. The Sheriff will ask that anyone who can help us by providing information as to Jake's last known whereabouts to come forward. He'll say Jake was found at the Mima Preserve under suspicious circumstances. He'll wrap it up with a statement that what happened is an isolated incident and there is no risk to the public. The Commissioner will then proclaim Mima Mounds open for the season. That's all that will be said publically right now."

"Okay. Got it." Now I know the party line. "Will they take questions?"

"No. Sheriff will address that up front."

We stepped out of the car. Carl leaned on the horn to get the Ranger's attention.

"You're kidding me. Tell me that's a pre-arranged signal and not a demonstration of your annoyance at the Ranger not coming in to your office?"

"A quick tap on the horn is universal language. Like knocking on a door, nothing more."

"We must come from different universes."

The Ranger, however, spoke Carl's language. He stood up to look from which direction the sound came then waved and started our way.

The cool air in the parking lot gave me a chill. I suggested we walk out and sit at a picnic table near the interpretive center kiosk away from the canopy of trees.

Approaching the kiosk, I now thought my original assessment of its resemblance to an alien space ship was spot on.

Dan and I sat. Carl remained standing and started the conversation.

"Ranger, ordinarily I do interviews at my office, but the powers that be thought it better to waste my time, not yours. I'm accommodating you and your boss this time; if we need to talk to you again, it will be downtown."

Dan fidgeted.

So did I. Carl's approach was not the format I had in mind.

Dan shifted around some before saying, "Am I a suspect?"

"Well, Ranger, we go through a process of elimination in this business, starting with the person who finds the body."

Yikes. Time to lighten it up. "Dan, how long have you been Ranger here? Is this your usual line of work? How does the Ranger business operate exactly?" I hit him with a few questions to encourage free-flow dialogue, hopefully, get him to relax a little.

"Umm, I started here in April. Before this, I had a job at the Mt. St. Helens Center. Worked up on the mountain three years. With the economy being what it is, cutbacks and layoffs came along. One of the Centers closed its doors altogether and they shortened up the season for the other Center. Saw a flyer announcing a position out here. Last guy had a heart attack or something and retired. He was well past the age to keep up with this kind of work."

I gave him a quizzical look. He explained further.

"Ranger duties involve a lot of bending, heavy lifting, and working outside in all kinds of conditions. Although this place is nothing like the snow and ice at St. Helen's, we had nice facilities to move out of the weather when we needed to. Here, all I have is a small space heater, window fan, an office the size of closet, and an even smaller restroom." He tossed his head back in the direction of the small buildings. "The position was posted as a one season, temporary. They're going to look at how to continue to staff it, I guess. Not sure what they'll do here after this." He lifted his chin in the direction where his wheelbarrow and shovel rested near the burial mound. "Anyway, I got the job. After this season, I think I'll try to get reassigned to St. Helens."

The work probably didn't involve removing gravesites up at St. Helens. Can't say I blamed him. I started thinking the land swap deal got sweeter for our County Commissioner with this incident.

"I take it this is your first body."

"Yeah. I admit I got a rush."

"How so?" Carl challenged.

"Oh. Well, I mean, well, um…"

I stepped in to prevent him going into a self-preservation mode resulting in the unwelcome outcome of him clamming up. "The name and picture of our victim were released today. Did you know him?"

"No. Never seen him before. But, he's like my age and size and all. It could have been me." His eyes widened as the realization hit him.

"You seemed pretty official out there with your little jars and all."

"I just wanted to help. This being my responsibility."

Carl jumped on that remark. "How so, Ranger Freis."

"I mean I work here, and it was done here, wasn't it?"

"Haven't determined that, yet."

Dan put his hands to his face and rubbed hard.

Carl pressed on. "Since our Coroner took his own dirt samples, what were you up to?"

Dan let out a long sigh. "I know it was wrong. I just wanted a little souvenir, that's all. I didn't take any bones or nothin'. Just some dirt. Something to tell the grandkids about someday, you know?"

"Actually. I don't," Carl said forcefully, moving closer to Dan. I want those jars turned over to me with anything else you might have taken to show the grandkids."

"Yes, sir. I have 'em right, right, over in my truck. I'll go get them."

"When I say, Ranger. When I say."

Critical point. The balance of power had tipped so far to Carl's corner it was time to even it out, or Dan was going to start calling for his lawyer or, worse yet, his labor rep.

"Dan, when you arrived for work, you were met by volunteers, you said. Anything about them strike you as strange? Ever seen any of them before?"

He reflected on the questions before speaking, noticeably relaxing as the focus shifted off himself.

"I don't think so. They all appeared to know each other. Said they'd been doing the same thing every May for years. This being my first season, no, I never ran into them before. They were friendly enough. Welcomed me to the *'Preserve Team'*, they called it."

Dan took off his Ranger cap and used his sleeve to blot the perspiration on his forehead.

Carl moved to his bottom line question. "Where were you during last year's Thanksgiving and Christmas holiday season?"

"I was housed with the other rangers up at the Mountain til we closed mid November. " I started here in April cleaning up storm debris and checking for encampments. We check for homeless folks, like every park does these days. I don't remember seeing anything unusual, but I wasn't looking for a new mound. The volunteers said it was just wrong in general. Didn't fit with the rest."

"And you were where during the holidays?" Carl moving back Dan back to his original question.

"Oh, yeah. I go skiing for two weeks over Christmas. Have since college. I'm always home for Thanksgiving. Mom's a great cook," his smile reminiscent of warm pumpkin pie. Stayed until March. Then, I came up here to find housing and get ready to take over this place from the previous Ranger."

"Should be easy enough to check on. Where 'bouts do you go skiing?"

"Bend, Oregon. Interesting territory there with great geological history."

"You camp or what?" Carl had no interest in the tourism log.

"No. I stayed with Mom and Dad from November through March. They live in Bend."

Dan sounded worn down. I felt like we were losing an important ally.

Carl wrote down the contact numbers for Dan's parents. He's never happy about blood relatives as alibis. They're unreliable, he tells me, not *'independent thinkers.* Carl seemed to have lost steam, or maybe just interest.

Ending every mediation session on a personal upbeat note, I decided to apply the same structure to this interview. "Dan, we were in Littlerock earlier. I didn't notice much by way of housing and this Preserve doesn't offer any, correct?"

"True. I found a little place in Tumwater, up the road fifteen minutes from here. I couldn't find anything closer."

"You're pretty much on your own working out here, aren't you?"

"Yeah. A good part of the time, I'm out in the fields with the tourists, doing guided tours, picking up, or making sure no funny business is going on. I got a radio if I need help. But, basically, my boss is in one location and I'm in a completely separate place. If I wasn't doing my job right, I'd hear about it," he said chuckling to himself. "Otherwise, yep, I'm on my own."

I felt creeped out thinking about having a job in such isolated conditions with a continuing stream of strangers. Not for me.

Carl wrote down the name and number of Dan's supervisor and put his notebook away. "If you remember anything that might help us out, please give me a call." He handed Dan his card, I was sure he's already done that, but he may be trying to make a point.

Dan took the card and said, "If there's nothing else, I really have to get back to work." He stood up to end this interview on his own terms. Good for him.

I looked at Dan, the wheelbarrow, and the massive dirt pile. A David and Goliath battle had its name all over that job.

Carl saw it too and took an instructive approach. "How far you haulin' the dirt, son?" You aware of how many trips it's gonna take to move it all out of here?"

"Don't I know it. Waiting on permission to bring the truck in. I found a spot for a couple small loads. I'm workin' over by those fir trees next to the fence. The rest will be hauled out in my truck."

"How about we get those dirt bottles from you. Then, we'll let you get on back to work." Adding his usual bit regarding interfering with a crime scene, the Ranger Dan Freis looked sufficiently admonished.

The three of us headed to the parking area. Dan retrieved the jars, handed them to Carl, and started back to the fields.

I wanted Dan back on our team, I said, "Say, Dan, it would help us to know how long it takes you to load the dirt into a truck. We'd have an idea how much time and effort went into this business," I said not wanting to name the deed.

Relieved to be back on the good guy's team and not the suspect team, his eyes lit up, he said, "You bet. I'll let you know."

Carl added, "Dan, I want to remind you this business of a homicide investigation is confidential. We aren't sharing any information other than what is released in our public statement."

"I understand. My boss already read me in. I'm not to comment on the matter in any way."

We thanked him and started our drive north. "You called him by name, he moving off your suspect list?"

"He's moving down my persons-of-interest list. I'm not done with Ranger Dan Freis or his story just yet."

CHAPTER 5

Waking early, I headed up the hill for a morning sauna. I saw Leon, exhibiting the patience of a saint, educating a member on the benefits of our recycling program rather than contributing to the County landfill. He gave me an extended high-five wave. I gave him one right back. He had his method of checking in with community members, this was ours.

Minutes later, the hot dry air sent my mind floating off to the place in my mind that I reserve for my favorite Detective, Bobby Goren. What would he think of Ranger Dan as a suspect? *'Motive, he'd ask first. What was his motive?'* I had to ask the same question about motive. Dan had nothing to gain. Next.

'Opportunity?' He *did* have an available truck and round the clock key access to move about without anyone paying much attention. Opportunity in spades.

'Evidence?' Seriously short in general with Dan or any other of our primary candidates.

And *'Means'*? I wasn't even sure what that meant.

I reminded myself Bobby looks outside motive, opportunity, evidence, and means. He looks for *brokenness*. People who snap one day, leaving families to sort out the mess they leave in their wake.

I do my share of dealing with brokenness. No one ever comes to mediation because they're having a good day.

Thinking it through, Dan's life appeared routine and comfortable. Dare I say, 'normal'? No hiccups. No brokenness. At least none I could see.

Relaxed and invigorated with my analysis of Dan as a suspect, I showered and dressed, then headed back home down the main road at a slow pace.

Upon opening my front door, I checked my cell and found a missed call and message. To be on the safe side, I'd left my cell phone behind. It may be a community here, but communities have all kinds of people; we were no exception. The message from Carl, twenty minutes ago, asked me to come in soon. It was now half past ten.

Already showered, I slipped out of sweats and into jeans and the almost clean pink T-shirt from the other day. I grabbed a fleece jacket, not taking any chances. With the warm spring sun making its presence, the County will be firing up the AC for the duration of good weather. Funny people, the rain people.

I did a five-minute blow on my hair. Mostly dry, I styled it with a comb and a little gel. It would dry in place on the trip downtown.

I stopped at Subway and was first in the door as they opened. I built a pair of meat trio foot longs, complete with Sun chips and apple juices and was on my way again in minutes.

Arriving in Carl's office just after eleven, his appreciative eyes told me he was both hungry and pleased we wouldn't be breaking for lunch. He pointed to the conference table and met me there. We didn't stand on ceremony and dug in. Half way through, Dr. Bob rapped on the open door.

"Carl. Lynzee. Thought you'd want to know I have my results on the ground ivy we found in the victim's mouth. Mind if I interrupt?"

"Come on in, Doc." Carl motioned him to the clearer end of the table not encompassed by our sandwich wrappings.

"Ground ivy has an interesting record." He flipped through

his notes with his index finger and launched into a dissertation. "This ivy is referred to as '*Creeping Charlie*'. Fatal to grazing horses if consumed in large amounts. Symptoms include," raising his eyebrows for affect, "breathing difficulties." He picked up his copy of the final autopsy report, flipping through the first several pages and continued, "Ground ivy poisoning is not common in people unless you happen to have some allergy to it. We didn't find evidence of any other toxins."

"Are you saying it did have a lethal effect on Jake?" Carl looked at the lettuce on his sandwich as he asked the question.

"This substance was not a factor in his death. So, my original findings stand." Doc looked up from his notes and said, "At the stage of decomposition we found him, there's not much else useful to be discovered other than what is already in my report. That said," he added, "ground ivy can be found as part of spiritual herb potions. The consequences of overdosing on a batch of herbs might, and I mean '*might*', result in some of the signs found in horses: swelling of the tongue, anaphylactic shock as a worst case. . ."

Summing up Doc's information, Carl said, "Jake ingested enough of the stuff to affect his breathing, catching him off guard. The advantage went to the killer then, and lights out," slapping his hands together as if controlling an off -on motion light to make his point.

I winced at the visual picture I now associated with Carl's clapping sound. I was relieved to see he'd put his sandwich down before his lights out demonstration.

"Well, yes," Doc responded. "Ingested in what, with what else, how much, and for what reason, I don't have the evidence to answer that question. I'll leave you to your lunch, then." He waved a goodbye.

"That adds a new aspect to the case, doesn't it?" I wrapped up the remains of my sandwich. My appetite had left the room midway through Doc's report. "Someone familiar with poisons or, at the very least, herbs is involved."

Carl made a quick note to his file. "Let's see here. We're looking for an herbalist, a medical professional, or someone trained in special ops. Or some combination."

"The more we learn, the less we know."

Another rap at the door. Carl waved in the officer. "What have you got for me, Tom?"

"Jake's friend, Paul Dobson, is in room four. Seems pretty busted up. Wants to share all he knows about Jake's whereabouts in December."

Carl stood up. Lunch was over for him, too. "Thanks. We'll head in."

Tom moved off back to his desk.

Carl put his hand on my shoulder as we walked down the hall. "You take the lead. Okay with you?"

"Sounds good." I stopped part way down the hall to ask, "From what Tom said, death must have occurred in December then, not November."

"So it would appear."

Staging area numbered doors lined the corridor, all referred to as 'interview rooms'. The nicer furnishings with comfortable chairs were behind door numbers three and four, the one we headed to, nicely appointed.

Room numbers one and two, not so nice. Worn out stuff went into the first two rooms, generally known to those who had reason to be inside as 'interrogation rooms'. Anyone coming back for a second 'interview' would likely find themselves moved to the less comfortable quarters at the front of the hallway.

We opened the door and found a young man, face riddled with grief. Seeing Paul Dobson answered my question about the quality of friendship that had existed between himself and Jake. Unshaven and uncombed light brown hair. His shoulders sagged and puffy brown eyes further evidenced his grief. His demeanor looked out of character for his stature of nearly six feet tall and two hundred pounds. Struggling to hold his solid frame together, it was clear Jake and Paul had been through life stuff together.

I glanced in Carl's direction and saw he noticed it, too. He would go easy; at least in the beginning. I breathed a sigh of relief and started us off. "Paul, I'm so sorry for your loss. You were close?"

"We were best buds. We hit the gym together three times a week after we discharged from the Army. Went out for beers. Friend stuff, you know?"

Carl and I both nodded that we did know.

Paul continued, "I started college last fall through the GI Bill. Jake wanted to work with his hands before he went back to school. Said he was going to put a year in the real world and then see what he wanted to do."

"You served together?"

"We did our bit in Iraq. Got back and got out together." His eyes watered as he said, "I can't believe he's dead. What happened? They said *'suspicious circumstances'* in the news."

I made a note to get a copy of the press release for future use.

Carl hesitated, and then answered, "Yes, that's true."

"That means someone had something to do with his death, right? Who did this?" His body became rigid. He tightened his hands to fists. "Better hope I don't get my hands on him before you guys do."

Not wanting Carl to mistake his expression of loss mistaken as a threat, I said, "Let's start at the beginning. What kind of work did you and Jake do in Iraq? Special ops?"

"No. We were in transportation. Ran supplies back and forth to our forward post guys."

"When did you last have contact with Jake?"

"Week before Christmas, we got together for a beer and pizza at the Cloverleaf in Tacoma. I told him I decided to go home to South Carolina to spend time with my family before winter quarter started up in January."

Something was off, other than my sudden craving for pizza. I'm a Cloverleaf addict. "That's great pizza and a fun place."

"Yeah. We hung there quite a bit."

"It sounds like it was unusual for you guys to not see each other regularly."

"What? Oh, no. Well. Yes. You see, he got himself hooked up with this girl, Brooke. Met at a party on base. He and I started seeing less of each other after that. When I got back in town in January, I found a note under my door telling me he took a construction job out of state. Wasn't til March break I got to wondering what was going on with not hearing a word from him." He paused weighing whether to continue.

"Paul, what aren't you telling us?"

He sighed. "I thought Brooke was trying to keeping him all to herself. I called her. I wasn't very friendly. She told me they broke up, but I didn't buy her story that he simply skipped out. Not on me, or his dad, without a word. She didn't like my attitude and hung up on me."

"Jake didn't have a cell phone?" Carl put his pencil down and read from the list of questions he'd generated.

"Not that I know of. We never needed one in the Army."

"Was it like him to leave you a note?"

"Not a note, exactly. It was a New Year's card. That's a special holiday for our unit. Since we weren't going to spend this one together, he must have decided to do the card thing. It was nice."

"You didn't report him as missing, though?"

"You don't go around reporting an Army buddy as missing. Not cool. I decided to talk to his dad and see what he knew."

"What happened?"

"Mr. Mathews was having the same concerns I was. I gave him Brooke's number. He didn't get very far with her, either, until he told her his next step was to file a missing person's report. Then she spilled that he had broken up with her; so, she hadn't been trying to find him."

I was finding this disappearance story disturbing. "Did Jake's dad file a report?"

"I don't know, I thought so."

Still puzzled, Carl continued. "I gotta tell you, it's a bit strange. You say you last saw your best bud a week before Christmas, and it's now May, and you didn't do anything about it."

"We had a disagreement over that girl. I told him she was wrong for him. She wasn't right, period."

I wanted to know what that meant, but Carl jumped in again.

"When did you fly east?"

"Christmas afternoon."

Sitting back in his chair, Carl spoke in his official voice, "Son, you better tell us if you know anybody who spent time with him after you did. This doesn't look good what with the fight between you and Jake."

Paul's eyes grew large, "Oh, geez. I loved the guy. I was trying to save him from making a serious mistake."

"Is that a confession?"

"What? No. Why are you saying these things?"

I reached out placing the palm of my hand on the table, patting it once lightly. His eyes came back to me. "We have to ask these kinds questions of everyone, Paul. We're trying to find out what happened to Jake and when."

He took a deep breath and exhaled, looked up, and nodded for me to continue.

"Tell me what wasn't right about Jake's relationship with Brooke, exactly."

He took a moment to gather his thoughts looking as though he was trying to decide how to say what he wanted us to know without digging himself in any deeper. Then, something inside told him to let it all out. "She was a piece of work. First of all, how they started dating, if that's what you call it. You hear about that?"

We indicated the negative, leaning forward preparing for an interesting story.

"She's a witch, for starters. I don't mean how she acts, she really is. A Wiccan, she says. Like I said, they met during this party."

Carl made a note, heavily underlining the word *'Wicca'* and smacked his pencil down. I wondered if, because of his Christian faith, he was wrestling with having this new Wicca angle in our investigation. Wanting to monitor how he was going to fare on this topic, I turned my chair slightly to keep him in view.

Paul had more to share regarding his best friend and Brooke. "She married Army. Not to someone we hung with," he explained. "Her husband hung himself 'cause he didn't measure up to her standards. Least that's what was going around." He shifted forward in his chair and continued. "Then, get this. During his funeral, she hooks up with Jake."

"Hooks up?" I asked to clarify what I think I already guessed.

"Gettin' it on in her car at the funeral home parking lot right after the service. Said the grief got to her; she needed to be close to someone. Haw."

Carl moved us off this subject and fast. "Yep. Some story, all right, Paul. I agree with you on that one. But, it still doesn't prove Jake was alive and well after you saw him," reminding him of the original problem.

"The four of us spent Thanksgiving at his dad's house. The three of them were making plans to spend Christmas season together when I left. You should talk to the witch. She probably put one of her spells on him and had him sacrificed under a full moon. Wouldn't surprise me. Her and her Coven, she calls 'em, aren't right in the head, none of 'em."

As much as I hated to admit it, until we corroborated his whereabouts Christmas Eve and Day, Paul would remain at the top of our persons of interest list, wrong as it felt. Something was still off. "You said you didn't know him very well, Brooke's husband, I mean. Why go to his funeral?"

"Mark was in our unit. All of us still around showed up. We would for anyone in our unit."

"Is there anyone that comes to mind who may not have liked Jake *'hooking up'* with Brooke like that?" Carl may have wanted to leave this subject far behind, but I saw motive here.

"I suppose there could be, but I never heard about it."

"Okay. What was Mark's job in the Army?"

"Medic. They deal with shit we only read about. You hear stories; not all of them come home with the same mind they took overseas with them. He mostly kept to himself in and out of the Service."

Carl abruptly changed the subject. "Any idea where Jake was working?"

"He worked in construction on the hotel going up behind that bird restaurant in Lacey."

At least Carl knew what he meant. "You mean Hawk's Prairie?"

"Yeah. That's it."

Continuing his post service line of questioning, he asked, "Did he have any enemies at the job site you know of?"

"Only the one. Brooke. He just didn't know it."

"Okay, Paul. I think that's enough for now. I'd like you to keep yourself available if we have any more questions. I'm going to send an officer in to collect names and places to establish an alibi for you so we can formally eliminate you from our investigation. We'll need to cover the week before Christmas through New Years."

"Okay." Paul lowered his head, fatigue taking its toll.

Carl closed the file, preparing to close the interview. He stood and put on a softer face, "Paul, whatever happened to Jake, we'll find who is responsible. You focus on school not revenge." He took a deep breath and spoke again in a sterner voice. "I have to insist that you do not discuss this case with anyone, publically, right now, difficult as that may be for you. We want every advantage catching the person responsible."

Paul almost saluted, but gave a hard nod instead.

"I want you to consider talking to your pastor or other spiritual care professional. You should not be carrying this load all on your own, son."

We hadn't talked about family yet. It was now or never. It fell to me.

"Paul, before we go, what can you tell us about Jake's relationship with his father?"

"Perfectly normal. Never had a bad thing to say about his father. His dad was kind and gentle toward Jake."

I met Carl at the door. We thanked Paul for coming in, adding our goodbyes. Carl opened the door, leaned out, and motioned to Tom. He sprinted toward us. Carl and I walked out and closed the door. Carl filled Tom in on what he wanted. Tom then entered the interview room, closing the door behind him. We headed back to Carl's office.

"Carl, I know it looks bad, but I don't think Paul's our killer. You don't keep each other alive in Iraq to come back home and kill your best friend over a girl you think is wrong for him."

Carl agreed but from a different perspective. "She's Wiccan. He may have wanted to kill *her*, but not Jake."

There it was. "Why do you say that?"

"Lynz, Paul wore a cross around his neck. No way he's going to support Jake being involved with her nor would he have any interest in her himself."

Okay. Good on him for noticing, I think. "You look for crosses on people, do you?"

"Not so much. But, he was pretty wound up talking about Wicca, and I thought that might be the reason."

"How about you? You wound up talking about Wiccans?"

"Not personally, as far as people go. I don't support what she calls 'faith' in any way. In case you're wondering, I wouldn't marry one."

"Would you marry a non Christian?" That came out wrong. I had no take backs with Carl and no time for self-correcting.

"No. That would be a deal breaker." He waited for me to comment.

Do I say I'm a baptized Episcopalian? Since I wasn't looking for a husband, I decided to keep my relationship with a higher being to myself. "I ask because I want to know how much your biases could affect this case."

"I wouldn't call it a *'bias'*. Personal preference, yes." He stopped outside his office door, standing within arm's length of my personal space.

I felt his eyes on me waiting to see how far I was prepared to pursue this subject of *'deal breakers'*. Not very. I started perspiring and hoped it wasn't showing. I changed the subject. "You were pretty hard on Paul. Yet, I'm sensing he's not high on your suspect list."

"Maybe I was a bit hard on him. Had to flush him out."

"Ah. Did it work?"

"I'll know when I see how his alibis check out."

"Do you think this murder is some kind of religious relationship or act gone wrong?" I put on my best *'all business'* face.

"I don't think we should rule it out." He wasn't moving one inch.

What to do. I'll keep changing the subject. "I'll do a little research on Wicca before we meet with Brooke."

Giving up on me saying something about my position on faith preferences in committed relationships, he stepped back, opened the door, and went to his desk.

Phew.

He wasn't finished with relationships yet. "You spending time in the family shrine these days?"

Ahh, this subject again. "It's not a shrine, Carl. I don't treat the cabin, nor do I use it, like a shrine. That would mean burning a bunch of candles, engaging in prayer, and whatnot. No."

"What is it then?"

"It's a workshop, mostly. And a place of family re-enactment."

"Like that civil war stuff where they all dress up in period costumes and shoot old rifles?"

If I didn't know him better, I'd say he was messing with me. "No. More like an interactive hobby shop. Drop it, please. I'm fine," my tone warning him to move on. "What's next?" I didn't know if I was staying or done for the day.

Out of the corner of my eye, I watched him mimicking the

words '*interactive hobby shop*'. Shaking his head in disbelief, he filed it away with other things he thinks peculiar about me and said, "Next? A meeting with dad, Mr. Mathews."

He wadded up the remains of the lunch we'd left behind earlier, triumphantly tossing them into the waste can. A victory shot.

That's why he brought up the '*shrine*'. My not being a graduate of the local law enforcement training academy, he feels the need to check on me, in his own way, during investigations to see how I'm doing at keeping the life of a case at 'arm's length', he says, from my own life story.

Wishing for more time to prepare myself before diving into another emotionally charged meeting, I'd just told him all was well. No way out of meeting with Jake's father now. "Good. Let's do it," now that I'd been played. So here we go. Turning, I lead the way to room three, solely to show him his little test was for naught. I stopped in front of the door, allowing Carl to open it. Protocol. I told myself.

A grief-ridden man of sixty plus years, struggled to his feet.

Carl motioned him back to his chair seeing the emotional and physical strain on our guest.

"Sir, my name's Carl Watson. This is Lynzee Rose. Together we make up the primary investigative team looking into your son's death. I want you to know we are doing everything in our power, with all our available resources, to bring to justice whoever did this."

He leaned across the table and shook hands. "I appreciate anything you can do, I really mean that."

I was already near tears, and we hadn't made it passed introductions. "Let me first say how sorry we are for your loss. To lose a child, well I can't imagine anything worse."

"Thank you, Miss. I'm Joe. Joe Mathews, Jacob's father." He set a shoebox-sized container on the table. "I brought photos and papers like you asked. Jake had 'em stored at my house. He'd been staying at my place after he discharged from the Army."

Calculating dates over six months ago made me wish I had last year's pocket calendar on me. "How long ago was that, sir?"

"About a year now. Though, I didn't see much of him once he started his new job. We got to seeing each other more regular when it ended in November, around Thanksgiving, I think it was." Joe's eyes were watering up. His hands pushed his memories box toward Carl.

Carl pulled it to him and began sorting through it, pulling out a small piece of paper. "This the outfit he worked for?"

Joe examined the payroll stub, holding onto it as he spoke. "Yeah. That's them. Now, I remember it was some hotel chain construction job."

Distracting him while Carl sorted through the items in the box, I asked, "Did Jake like the construction work he was doing at the hotel? Unlike the work he did in the Army, I'd guess."

"Yes, ma'am. He said it was a good gig. Long hours, but good people. He especially liked it every payday. Good money."

"I can only imagine how much you miss him. Did you spend Christmas with Jacob?"

"We spent time together Christmas Eve morning. It's always been a hard day for us without his mom here. Holidays are never the same without her."

That piece of timeline may have moved Paul further down our list.

I wished I could fast-forward those thirty days from Thanksgiving to Christmas for all us grievers. I asked, "Did he seem different this particular Christmas holiday as compared to others?"

"Well, now that you mention it, he did seem to have a sparkle in his eye." He burst into tears.

I pushed the tissue box in his direction.

Carl jumped up and returned with a bottle of water.

We sat quietly, waiting until he was ready to continue.

"I didn't even ask him about it." His muffled response came from inside his own handkerchief. Joe's grief was now intermixing with guilt, a by-product of loss.

Time to redirect. "Tell us about Thanksgiving. Paul said you all spent some fun time together."

"You know, that was a real nice time. He brought this girl around." He pulled the box back to him and reached in, pulling out a photograph. "Took this picture on Thanksgiving Day with one of those remote control camera things. See. That's me, and that's Jacob." He turned the picture toward himself then back to us. "That's his friend, Paul. His family's back East so he spent the day with us. And the girlfriend, Brooke's her name, standing next to Paul. I don't think she had family around either. Yeah, we had a real nice time." He held the picture out to me.

I took the picture, studying it, hoping it would speak to me in a way I could use to work this case. Good-looking kid. Blue eyes, light hair, tan, solid build. Definitely in the heart breaker category. Looking closer, I saw that both Jake and Paul wore crosses around their necks. I started to ask about Jake's faith, but Carl moved us away from the holiday season.

"Did Paul and Brooke get along?"

"Paul was polite. Didn't seem to care much for her. Put up with her 'cause Jacob liked her."

"Did you ever meet any of the guys he worked with at the construction job?"

"No. Never did. Called Christmas Eve afternoon to tell me he was picked to work out of state with the construction crew. Said he would let me know as soon as he got settled."

"Did he call you from a cell phone?" Carl still working the angle of tracking down phone records.

"Don't know. He didn't have one of his own. Never been very good at managing money. Told him he could use my cell phone while he was gone so's he could keep in touch. I don't use it much. I have a landline works well enough for me, anyway. He said this gig was gonna put him ahead on his bills enough so's he could buy a cell and some other toys."

Seeing a healing opportunity, I asked, "You think that sparkle you saw in his eye on Thanksgiving could be the news he was expecting to be picked to be part the extended crew?" More importantly, I hoped to help take some of the guilt off this poor man's shoulders.

"Yeah. That was probably it. Yeah. He was happy." He smiled softly to himself.

"Joe," Carl back on track with the other side of relationships, "You ever see a fight between Paul and Jake?"

"Naw. They'd argue, like friends do over football teams and such. In fact, we watched a game together Thanksgiving Day. They enjoyed sparring with each other."

Wanting to learn more about the relationship between father and son, I asked, "If you had to describe Jacob's qualities, what would they be?

Beaming for the first time, perhaps in days, he said, "That's easy. Kind. Gentle. Honest blue eyes. Soft smile and an engaging way about him. Not much of a partier for a kid his age. He did love a good microbrew, though. Said he wanted to start making beer; had an idea of creating his own personal brand. Not being a beer drinker myself, we didn't talk much more about that. Brooke seemed to be real interested in home brews, if you know what I mean," he made circle motions around his ears, rolling his eyes at the same time.

Careful not to imply Brooke was a suspect, but anxious for dad's view of his son's relationship, I asked, "What do you think of Brooke?"

"She was nice enough. Seemed to like Jacob. I didn't meet her 'cept the one time. Said she was a vegan. A hard thing to be at a Thanksgiving dinner," he gave a small chuckle to himself. "But, she was a good sport about it. We had enough side dishes to make a plateful for any vegetable eater."

"We don't have a last name for Brooke. You happen to know it?" Carl asked as he stood up.

"Can't say if I ever knew it or just plain forgot."

"Joe, I'm going to have one of my detectives begin putting some pieces together with all this stuff you brought in. I'm sure we can use the Thanksgiving picture here," waving the photo in the air, "to help us find a full name for Brooke." He put the photo back in the box with the rest of the photos, trinkets, and assorted documents. "You okay to leave them with us for a bit. We'll take real good care of these."

I squeezed his hand as added assurance.

"Yeah. Anything, if it helps find out what happened to my boy."

Carl crossed over to the wall phone. "Bill, come down here when you can. We have a photo of the girlfriend. See if you can ID her from it. First name's confirmed. We also have a box of things here that might be of some help in learning more about Jake's movements last winter."

Bill appeared moments later. He walked across and reached out his hand to Joe, "It's an honor to meet the father of a soldier, sir."

That single gesture brought Joe to a full upright, proud parent, seated position. Joe grasped his hand, thanking Bill for his kind words. He took the box, nodded in our direction, and left the room.

Bill just made a permanent impression on me, too.

Returning to his chair, Carl folded his hands in front of him, resting them informally on the table. "Joe, tell me again. When was the last time you and Jake saw or spoke to each other?"

Joe took a swipe at his silver hair with the palm of his hand. "He called Christmas Eve afternoon. That was the last time we spoke." His cheeks flushed.

Now a question I wasn't sure I wanted to know the answer to. "You hadn't spoken or seen your son for five months after that Christmas Eve call?"

"I know it seems strange. His being in the Army and all often put him out of touch with me. I was kinda used to it. When he took the out of state job, I figured he was just that, out of touch. When April came along, though, I decided something was wrong. I panicked and filed the report. I didn't think to call the hotel people."

Leaning forward searching Joe's face, Carl asked, "What report? I've checked. I didn't find a missing persons record?"

"I filed one with the Army."

We both sat up straight with a jerk nearly falling off our chairs.

I managed to get my voice back first. "Why the Army?"

"I thought it was the best place. I didn't mean any disrespect. But the Army does get results, you know," apologizing for his opinion of local law enforcement.

Carl made a cutting motion with his hand. "Never mind that. What did you learn?"

The door swung open and in came Detective Tom. He placed a file in front of Carl and left.

Carl raised his finger for Joe to wait while he scanned the verbatim typed interview with Paul Dobson.

Carl fought hard to keep this piece of his budget. Transcription of these sessions immediately upon completion.

A minute later, looking up, he asked, "You filed the report after talking to Paul, is that right? He called you?"

"Yeah, that's right. Told me he hadn't heard from Jacob in months, got worried, and then couldn't get any information out of Brooke. It was after I talked to Brooke when I decided to file a report."

Carl closed the file, all ears and asked, "What exactly did Brooke say that convinced you Jake was missing?"

"She said she hadn't seen him during her Yule celebration. She thought they were going to be spending time with each other during both holidays, his and hers. Seems she came to the conclusion Jake decided her religion wasn't going to work for him, Jacob being a Christian."

I was having a hard time keeping track of who talked to who when. "So, you spoke with Brooke after Thanksgiving Day?"

"Only the one call back in March. She was a nice enough gal. Her not eating meat was gonna wear Jake down soon enough. I knew

I wasn't gonna see any grandkids from that relationship. After I hung up the phone, it was time for me to find some answers."

Carl pulled a little yellow sticky off the file, read it, and then crumbled it up. "Her name is Brooke Rivers."

I raised my eyebrows wondering if her middle initial was "S" for Stream. Her parents were either nature buff s or she changed it along the way. But, back to the missing person's report. "What did you find out from the Army?"

"I met with the base commander. Jacob discharged himself from the Army so, technically, he said he couldn't help much. Agreed to have the Military Police poke around, talk to some of the guys in his unit, and see if anything useful turned up. He called back and told me he talked to the Base Chaplain, too. Nothing came of any of it. Said Jacob hadn't applied for vet benefits, either." He drew in a deep breath, letting his shoulders drop.

"I'm sure you're exhausted," looking over at Carl. He gave a quick nod in agreement. "We're finished for now. Can we help you with anything, Joe, besides finding what happened to your son?" Empathy creeping out of my pores, I pondered whether facing my own grief with others, instead of harboring it like a silent martyr, might be worth a try.

"I'm on my way to meet with the County Doc next. Arranging for Jake to be taken over to the Base for a special Memorial Day service. His troop took up a collection. He'll be buried on base. Nice of 'em and all."

"Very special, indeed. All right then, sir."

We all stood up together.

Carl said, "We'll be in touch. I have to insist you not discuss this case publically with anybody, difficult as it may be, including how we found him, Joe. Our only hope is to catch up to the person responsible without scaring off anyone connected. Okay?"

"Sure. Sure. I understand."

"I'd like to encourage you to take part in some grief or spiritual counseling. It may not seem like much right now, but I know it helps."

That was nice, I thought.

We walked out together. Ushering Joe to the elevator, I pushed the button and guided him into the elevator. His movements were slow; his lack of sleep, combined with grief and stress, were all catching up to him.

We stopped long enough to grab fresh coffee. We were halfway down the hall when Carl's desk phone started ringing off the hook. He jogged in and grabbed hold, listening with a dumbfounded stare. Sitting down hard, searching my face, and the phone now pressed against his chest, he said in a weak voice, "Jake's remains are missing."

"He's gone?" I shrieked in disbelief. I would have fainted on the spot, but I'd never see this case through to the end if I did that. I sat down fast before I fell down.

Carl tapped on his window for Tom and Bill's attention, waving them into the office. From the look on his face, they sprinted in. He briefed them. The shock showing on their faces as well. He put the phone back to his ear, took a deep breath, and said, "Doc, we're on our way." We all charged toward the elevator leaving our steaming cups of hot coffee behind.

CHAPTER 6

THURSDAY, MAY 26TH

Still able to visualize yesterday's blur of activity, I saw friends' voices raised against each other and arms flailing in frustration, making my head spin even now. The taking of Jake's remains meant we were no longer looking at a simple murder, if there is such a thing. The act solidified relationship, ritual, or both.

I shifted into overdrive when the elevator doors opened and I saw Joe, collapsed on the hallway floor. Bill, Tom, and Carl ran off, all in different directions. I sat with Joe until the Medics arrived to work their magic. I listened as Doc told Carl what had happened. He'd gone to ready his son's remains for pickup and transport and discovered they were gone. He'd asked Joe if he had made other arrangements for Jake. Joe shook his head then slumped to the floor. Other than seeing a good-sized bump on his head and an oxygen mask affixed to his face, I didn't hear if there was a further diagnosis, the medics weren't making one.

I rode in the ambulance; Joe's hand clamped on mine making any other choice awkward. He was pale. His skin clammy. I tried to assure him it was a simple mix-up; everything would be all right. As the ambulance pulled away, I glanced out the back window to see Carl and Doc staring at each other in complete disbelief at what this could mean.

Once Joe was checked into the hospital, I went home, poured a glass of wine, and took to searching online for information on Wicca: practices, potions, and history. I couldn't think of anything else to do with myself, and doing this helped me distance myself from the earlier horror. Carl will need this information, I told myself, even if it isn't going to be our first priority of the day. I finished then sank into a winged back chair, my thinking chair, and woke the next morning in the very same spot, no wiser.

Finishing a second cup of vanilla infused coffee was the first part of my replenishment program for today. Part two, a trip to the cabin for a little C & R, Connection and Reflection, that is.

Savoring the brew, I walked outside to my cabin. Once inside, tendrils of memories tugged at my heartstrings; memories of my own family banding together when I was young, pulling one or more of us along through trying times. It was the overwhelming number of challenges that took its toll on our family unit, leaving only its individual members to fend for themselves.

I stepped outside and sat down on the small porch to watch the morning unfurl. The breeze moved through trees, the sound reminiscent of the rustling of ladies' skirts moving along the promenade of a long ago time. Taking a deep breath, I exhaled hoping for a message from the universe. Nothing.

The sun danced a Morse Code message inside cedar branches as the flickers of light broadcast an SOS aimed at my deep-seated abandonment issues. Message received. If I let myself be drawn in emotionally today, I'll pay the price later. Proceed with caution, Lynzee.

With only a half hour I'd given myself to refuel, it was time to proceed to Carl's office. I called him and let him know I was on my way.

I put my parking pass on the dash as I drove into the County lot. I didn't always use it, but an hourly use rate would add up fast today. I expected to be here all day til sundown.

The day before a long holiday weekend, I knew no one in the

Homicide Division would be enjoying any part of it until Jake's remains were back where they belonged, in the morgue.

The third floor radiated a ghostly quiet, causing me to wonder about my earlier theory. I hurried through to Carl's office and looked back at the array of empty desks, confused. Moments later, he appeared and motioned for me to follow him, his Mona Lisa smile now upside down.

We walked in silence to a small auditorium. A wall screen activated as we entered. He motioned for me to sit next to him .A few detectives lined the wall; others dispersed themselves in seats around the auditorium. The video technician popped a VCR tape into the player and waited for word to roll the tape.

I concentrated on relaxing my shoulders; I'd have a serious neck ache at the end of today if I didn't. Another part of my plan to stay centered.

"What's this? Where'd someone come up with a VCR tape? I thought they were all but extinct, Carl?"

"It's my tape from home I made for the case file. I may be a dinosaur on some things, but I'm hardly extinct," Carl said while putting his fingers to his lips lest I be thinking about some comeback. I wasn't. Not today. Carl gave a nod.

The screen jumped into action. The press conference came to life. The Commissioner and County Sheriff were together facing their constituents.

The Sheriff led off by reporting a young man's body was discovered in the Mima Mounds Preserve and has been identified as Jacob Mathews. He asked that anyone who had information about Jacob's movements last December to contact his office. He finished by saying the public is not at risk as this case appears to be an isolated incident.

Next, Commissioner Whittier stepped to the microphones and spoke of the history of the Mounds, assuring her audience no damage occurred to this special place. She finished by announcing that Mima Mounds Preserve was officially open for an early start to the season. She then turned, motioning to someone standing in the sidelines.

Joe Mathews stepped to the podium. Carl leaned forward. I pressed myself back in my seat, experiencing the same sensation you feel speeding down a runway right before liftoff. Joe stared into the camera, and spoke passionately. "I will miss my son so much. My boy will be transported to Ft. Lewis Cemetery where the men he served with in Iraq and I have arranged for a military burial."

"Shit." Carl flew up from his theater style chair. Pacing back and forth, he grabbed at a wall phone. After some foul language for him, he slammed it down and turned back to all of us.

"That," pointing to the screen, "is why this department and public relations are like apples to oranges."

I'm not sure what it was supposed to mean, but this was not the time to ask for clarification. He went on to tell us that the PR department came up with this *'asinine'* idea to refocus attention from the crime scene to an actual Memorial Day military service. Inadvertently, they broke a cardinal rule; delicate information had been released during an open investigation.

"Carl, the good news in all this is the killer is still here; this was a local broadcast not a national one." My voice echoed throughout the silent auditorium.

He stopped scowling long enough to let it sink in. Turning to the technician, he said, "Put in the feed from the entrance to the morgue. Start with Tuesday noon through Wednesday noon." He looked around til he spotted his top team members. "Tom. Bill." They stepped forward from the wall where they had plastered themselves. "You two stay and study this video with Doc. He's on his way up. Look for anyone coming or going that doesn't belong. Check for someone leaving with a bag or container large enough to hold the skeletal remains of a grown man. When you find it, call me. I'll be in my office." He turned, moving quickly out of the room.

I followed. If he didn't want me with him, I'd know soon enough.

Coming toward us were Doc and the staff person on duty when the discovery was made. None of us spoke or made eye contact. My neck started throbbing. The office door slammed shut as I squeezed through. I sat down and waited. I didn't have to wait long.

Shouting, Carl demanded, "Talk to me. Tell me about Joe."

"I had a call from the hospital on my way here. He asked the hospital staff call me. He suffered a mild heart attack, but it looks like he's going to make it. A couple of men from his grief-counseling group, more like just friends of his, are with him, arrived first thing this morning. We might want to stop by and check on him sometime today."

"And say what? Sorry we couldn't keep your son *or* his remains safe?"

I blinked, hard. He was venting. Venting is good. It beats the alternative of punching a whole in the wall. I continued to wait him out, or at least wait til he sat down.

He paced about. After a few minutes, taking a deep breath, he took a seat across from me making piercing eye contact. His brown eyes darkened. I could tell he was recalling the complete fiasco of a press conference and the inconceivable breach it caused.

"Well, no. I'm thinking we want him to know we won't sleep til we bring Jake back, or something along those lines."

He stared at me, the clock ticked away the seconds. As though an onstage curtain lifted, he let out a sigh, slapped his thighs with the palms of his hands, and stood up. "Okay. I agree. Although, I wouldn't call it good news. Somebody involved in this is in town all right." He turned suddenly and asked me, "Did you find out anything on Wicca? Brooke is coming in this afternoon. I want to know what it looks like. How it's organized. What they do and don't do. Worship and don't worship."

The string of sentences caught me by surprise. He usually rolled them out one at a time. I took the notepad from my bag; glad I'd followed my instincts last night and did the research. I started my report, "First, some history. Many years ago, the Wiccan faith went underground. They practiced in small groups called *'covens'* staying secretive until not all that long ago."

"Why the history lesson, Lynzee?"

"I think it's important since Brooke will be reluctant to share information with us outsiders."

He rolled his eyes at me.

Persisting with making my position on this matter understood, I said, "We have to tread lightly on this subject, Carl, if you expect to get anything useful out of her. I want to see you put those Christian values of yours, like patience and tolerance, into practice when you're interviewing her. And, remember, this is an interview, not an interrogation."

His body language told me he wasn't enjoying my lecture. His eyes, however, didn't disagree with me.

"Let me say after what I've learned about them, I don't think this murder would occur by the coven as a whole; their overriding commandment, or golden rule, is *'do what you want as long as it doesn't harm anyone'*. Sound familiar?" I didn't wait for an answer. "A self-serving version of the original we know, yes? However, Wiccans do not promote wrongdoing. None of the rituals I found disrespect any life form: animal, plant, or being."

"That does not preclude somebody with a personal vendetta acting outside the rule though, does it?"

"Let me put it this way. In my line of work, it comes down to a matter of issues and interests. If the issue is joining the Wicca faith, then the interest is to bring Jake into the Wiccan community, not kill him. See what I mean?"

"Only true if *that* is the issue. Could be plain old-fashioned personal betrayal or jealousy. Wicca principles aside."

"Well, there is another piece to think about. The practice of magick and ritualistic ceremony is part of what makes up the Wicca faith."

Carl cringed at my use of the word *'faith'*, but I persisted.

"They utilize herbs. Here's where we get Brooke to help us.

Jake was her boyfriend. Let's make her our ally in unraveling this ground ivy thing. Maybe she can shed some light. Maybe she knows someone who uses it or knows where to buy it."

"Anything else?"

"Yeah. The murder weapon. Wiccans make use of knives in their rituals, but none of their primary knives or tools that I found on the internet fit Doc's description of the murder weapon."

"What does this tell me?" Carl's frustration was showing again.

"Nothing they use in their rituals fits the wound an ice pick like object would make."

"You stay up all night?"

"As a matter of fact, I did not. Internet research is quite fast, you should give it a try."

Carl gave me the stink eye. I continued.

"You'll love this next part. Three words, Waning Moon Magic." I waited for applause but got only a wary look. I pressed on. "The waning moon is a time for ridding oneself of addiction, illness, or negativity." Again nothing. More staring. "The moon was in Leo on Christmas Eve and Christmas Day. Gatherings involved rituals of power over others."

"Now *that's* what I want to hear. Something we can use to scare the witchin' beegeebees out of her. Make her cooperate with us."

Seeing his sudden enthusiasm for my research findings, I concluded with, "And, drum roll, please. A particular ritual in December is Oak Moon. The focus is on the ancient oak with its trunk and branches in the material world of the living and its roots deep into the underworld."

"There aren't any oak trees in the prairie lands," his tone indicating he was not impressed with my finale.

"Symbolism, Carl. I know there aren't oak trees in the Preserve. What's important is the ceremony is tied to the earth's life and death cycles." I was about to share what I'd found about spiritual rituals that include bones, when Tom popped in.

"Sir, we're ready for you."

As we started out the door, I put my hand on his arm, "We mustn't let Joe know he basically told the killer everything he or she needed to retrieve Jake's remains. It would kill him."

Carl shook his head at the memory, nodding as we started down the hall.

All eyes turned to us as we walked in. The atmosphere in the auditorium was now thick enough to cut with a knife but an improvement from the chainsaw it would have taken earlier. I grabbed the first empty chair, Carl stood with his arms crossed.

"We have our culprit!" Doc exclaimed.

Carl took a deep breath and exhaled. Relief showed on his face. "Let's see what you have then." He gave a nod. The feed cued to the glass entrance doors. The divided hallway split, the left leading to the elevators, the other to the Morgue.

"Watch this." Doc rocked on his toes as he spoke.

I scooted to the edge of my seat in anticipation. A figure in a lab coat and skullcap walked toward the morgue. No way to tell if it was a man or woman. The eyes of this person remained focused on the floor, prompting me to think he or she knew enough to avoid making eye contact with the cameras. Without color images, the hair color, skin tone, and features were indistinguishable. The poor image quality did not improve no matter how much I squinted.

Doc paused the feed with the remote control and turned to face Carl. "It was Deputy Tom Ogg who spotted our villain leaving." He turned to Tom and said, "Tom, why don't you take it from here?"

Tom got up from his front row seat and stood alongside the screen. He took the remote from Doc and began. "I think we can all agree, it would be difficult picking anyone out of a line-up based on the image we've seen so far," nodding toward the frozen frame on the screen. "But, what you'll see next is the same person in this frame, dressed differently and leaving the building." He pushed the button. The feed rolled.

We watched as someone, roughly the same size and build, came into view wearing a jogging suit and carrying a large gym bag. Complete with IPod and ear buds, the image on the screen's head bent forward and bobbed, presumably, in sync to music, but the face remained hidden from the camera.

Tom's voice increased in intensity. "Look closely. The gait is identical to the earlier image of the person we saw entering the building. Perhaps an injury to the left leg."

I saw it. Sure enough, this person favored their left leg. Trying to disguise their appearance but having to deal with a walking limp. A breakthrough in the case.

"Good work, Tom." Carl turned to direct his next comment to Doc. "It doesn't explain how someone walked into the morgue unnoticed."

Doc lowered his eyes. "No. It does not. I *can* explain the limp."

This I had to hear. How could he do that from an image on a screen?

"From what I've been able to put together, a call came into my office reporting someone had collapsed outside. My staff jumped up to respond. Not accustomed to this type of call, they went out into the parking lot, leaving our area unattended."

"Why would someone call the Morgue and not 911?" This seemed to be an unusual occurrence. I was asking myself as much as the room. Doc responded.

"Exactly, Ms. Rose. It is very unusual indeed. I'm revising procedures to make sure our facility is never left unattended again." He turned to address Carl directly. "I'm sorry, Carl. It should never have happened."

Carl patted Doc on the back and the tension in the air took on a noticeable improvement. He asked, "What about the parking lot incident?"

"And the limp," I reminded him.

"Both real enough," Doc continued, "part of which was staged. Seems an innocent bystander, an elderly man, fell. Witness statements tell us he was knocked into from behind creating the distraction. However, both people fell, and were tangled up together. That was not part of the original plan, I expect. All the focus went to the older man; no one got a good look at the other person who limped off from the scene." Still not willing to let his own office off the hook, he repeated, "The phone call was a trick. We don't receive live assistance requests. Again, I'm sorry. It appears the incident was a ruse to get us out of our facility and our intruder into the building unnoticed. It worked, unfortunately."

"Alright. Let's print out copies of the photo. One of the person coming in and one of them leaving. Show it around the building to anyone on duty during the incident, we have the date and time it happened now. See if anyone remembers seeing this person." Carl walked to the door, then turned and added, "I'm sure I don't need to tell you, this incident is to remain out of the local news. No word of it leaves the building. Are we clear?" Nods came from every direction. Carl opened the door and started out, then turned back to his team and said, "Good work. All of you," letting his eyes settle on Doc.

He left, the door closing behind him. I followed, not sure of what was next, but increased my pace to catch up to him. "Another reason we might want to stop in and talk to Ralph, unless someone's already taking care of it?"

"Got it covered. The Sheriff wants to handle it personally. He'll explain to Joe just why keeping it quiet gives us the advantage over the thief who won't know he or she's been discovered. "

"What's next for today, Carl?"

"Lunch with my Pastor. You spent time on the internet. Now, we're going to do things the old-fashioned way. Talk to an expert on this spiritual stuff, including our missing bones."

"Good idea." I meant lunch, but I was game to meet the mysterious Pastor.

We met Michael Gordon at the Spar in downtown Olympia, a spot known for their particular brand of micro brews. The Spar became part of the renowned Portland, Oregon chain that crossed state borders, from consumer pressure, into Washington. Prior to bringing their product North, drinking a McMenamins Bagdad Ale, Cascade Head Ale, Crystal Ale or Ruby Ale made for a long drive.

The walk downtown felt great. We found Carl's pastor at a booth sipping, what smelled like, wonderful coffee. He waved us over. Rising as we approached, he held out his hand, "You must be Lynzee. Carl mentions you often. Seems he puts a lot of faith in your abilities. Call me Mike."

His well-trained handshake expressed sincerity. I found him even more handsome in person. "I recognize you from the poster in the hallway at your Church."

"Did that a make a good impression or a bad impression?"

"It raised some questions."

"It's a great story. Perhaps I'll have an opportunity to share it with you sometime."

We sat, Carl planting himself next to me. We ordered and stuck to coffee, though several brews going to other tables were tempting. While we waited for our lunch and then between bites of our specialty burgers, fries and special sauce, Carl briefed Mike on the case, beginning with the burial all the way to the theft, which I remembered was information that was not supposed to leave the building. Carl included many details. Things his Pastor would not hear at any press conference.

Noticing the look of concern on my face, he clarified, "I tell you all of this, Mike, because I'd like your input on a couple of points. Most of what I'm telling you will not be released to the public. I need to keep it that way."

"Of course. Anything you say to me stays between us. You know that Carl."

Hmmm. What did that mean?

"I was wondering about your choice of meeting places when you started talking," Mike said looking around him, "but I see that the high ceilings and open space actually do make private conversations possible."

"In retrospect, I probably should have met with you in my office. But, the food's better."

We all agreed that was a definite bonus.

"Well, Mike, now I have some questions for you. What might we be dealing with? A religious fanatic? A psycho? Witchcraft? Are we looking at Nisqually spiritual practices? Why take the bones? What known rituals tie together this killing, burial, and bone taking?"

Mike absorbed the flurry of questions faster than I did. He lowered his head and then spoke. "My first thought, from the events you described, is this crime is about relationship and ritual. Ceremony was involved. Both in the place selected for young Jake and in the manner of burial; the mound carefully formed to blend with surroundings."

He had our attention. Neither Carl nor I spoke. He continued.

"I'm not a detective, but it troubles me that Jake was buried fully clothed, personal items removed."

I jumped in. "I agree. Why did the killer hide the identity unless he or she wanted the personal items for some reason, like a trophy?"

"If the crime was a robbery gone wrong, the ceremony and burial site don't make much sense," Carl added.

Mike continued his line of reasoning. "I'd say the killer didn't expect the gravesite would be found. By retrieving the remains, the killer confirmed he didn't want him found." He frowned then said, "But why?"

The answer came to me. "Unless to bury him again."

Carl excused himself and stepped outside; cell phone pressed to his ear.

I took the sudden departure to try to learn a little more about his Pastor. "The photo of you in the poster was taken where?"

"Ahh," he broke into a wry smile, "Jerusalem. Led a youth group to Israel. The trip turned into a little more than our planned vacation. Right place at the wrong time. Or, maybe it was the right time. Anyway, we found ourselves mixed up in a Palestine border dispute. I learned, the hard way, it's best not to be on the wrong side of your homeland and allies when traveling to political hotspots. Things got a bit sticky. Just a misunderstanding, you understand. We all made it home safely."

I laughed. "Quite an experience for your youth group, I'd say." Probably enough on that. Carl might return any second. I was sure he wouldn't consider the topic dining material. "Carl tells me you've been here a year. Where's home?"

"Born in New Hampshire. I completed most of my education back east then moved west as my politics grew more liberal. Ended up in Oregon for my early pastoring years. First church was in Salem, Oregon, of all places. Fortunately, the town bore no resemblance in religious practices to its East coast namesake of historical fame. Christian Hope, here in Lacey, is my first church in Washington. And you?"

"Native of Western Washington. Grew up in Ruston, a small smeltering company town. Most of my working career I've lived in Tacoma. Not a church goer." I don't know why I put up the blockade, but I stopped trying to answer my relationship sabotage questions years ago.

"Not a problem, I've been there myself. And, in case you didn't know, it doesn't take a building to celebrate a relationship with God."

Before I could pursue that, Carl plopped down.

"Mike, we gotta wrap this up. Just need to finish where we left off talking about the removal of the bones. My question to you is this, what might it mean from a religious or ritual stand point?"

"If the intent was to move the bones at some later date, then I'd say ritual is part of what went down. If the site was to be the final resting place, I think we're looking less at ritual and more spiritual. At first blush, anyway, that's my theory."

I asked, "What if the killer wanted the body in a skeletal

state before removing it, the more time that passed with the body undisturbed, the better, right?"

Carl answered, "That's true. But why would that be important."

Mike said, "Well, Carl, if we go with Lynzee's scenario the intent was to remove the body at some later date, what comes to mind regarding bones is the Voodoo religion."

This was in line with what I had learned online last night.

"Ancestors are held in such high regard in the practice of Voodoo that some wear the bones of their ancestors in some fashion on their bodies or display them in the home."

Carl exhaled loudly. "Just what I need. Another religious faction to this homicide."

"I hear ya. I think you'd know, though, if there was a substantial Voodoo community in Thurston County. I don't know of any." Pastor Mike checked his watch, tapped it with a finger, and said, "I gotta wind this up soon, myself. Anything more you want to brainstorm with me?"

I felt we had a key missing element to this case. "We can't deny the bones, or Jake himself, mean something to the killer. They're either going back to Mima Mounds or to a safer more private area."

Both Carl and Mike turned to look at me and then nodded in agreement.

"Still," I said resolutely, "I don't think the body was ever supposed to be discovered."

Carl's face took on an uneasy look. "Ranger's is hauling dirt out as we speak. I'm concerned if the killer discovers his dirt's gone, it could put him and anyone visiting the Preserve at risk. I called to put a team back down there effective immediately til we put an end to this business."

"I'll pray on it, Carl."

I squirmed a little in my seat hoping it went unnoticed. He gets answers through prayer. I don't know if I'd know how to do it right. Praying always seemed a self-serving practice; asking for something for yourself from a higher being. Yet, the idea of communicating with God in the middle of a long sleepless night had its appeal, even at the-risk of no response. "Mike, I'm curious about your Church. Well, not about your Church, but about your building." There I go again, putting up my brick wall disclaimer. "About the shape mostly. It looks like a big concrete tent."

"You noticed! The story about the shape goes back to revival meetings, 'gospel crusades' as they were known. They date back to the eighteen hundreds. I don't know if Carl's shared much about our Church, we have an atypical way of doing things that are a bit outside mainline church models. We're still very much scripture based. Generous endowments allowed us to build our church in the model we aimed to emulate, the outdoor revival meeting of past days that were held under large tents."

"Like the circus tents?" I immediately regretted the comparison and changed the subject. "What's different about your church, if you don't mind my asking? Isn't it the same basic agenda: singing, Bible reading, sermon, passing the plate, praying…?"

"Agenda? Well, yes and no. The tent shape of our building is tantamount to the experience the traveling evangelists brought to towns. Celebration of a relationship with God and recruiting of new Christians. People heard the joyful noise coming from inside the tents, could see inside, and then choose to be part of it without the fear of the unknown that stepping inside a brick and mortar building might bring. The outside tent setting was open and relaxed. Easy to come and go. It just worked." He saw he hadn't lost his audience. He continued. "In today's world, we have downloadable sermons and cyber churches. Believers connect with each other online, or not at all in some formats. Our tent building is a throwback to an earlier time when church was about the gathering of community."

"Is it working? This new old style approach?"

"Why don't you stop in and see for yourself."

I walked right into that one. Mike had me right where he wanted me. Carl smirked keeping his eyes averted.

Coming to my rescue, Carl said, "Pastor, I'm afraid I gotta cut this short, too. You can take another go at her next time we see you."

Pastor Mike smiled. "It will be a pleasure."

We gathered up our bills, Carl took them from us saying it was his treat. I got a hug from the Pastor, surprising me but not Carl. We said our goodbyes, and Carl and I hurried back to his office to meet with the witch.

Carl was pondering something on our walk back. He decided to put it into words. He turned to me with a concerned look. "Pastor believes in hugging. Part of his community family emphasis. I should have warned you. You okay with it?"

Carl's mandatory department sensitivity training was showing. "No problem," still processing how I really felt about it.

*   *   *

Brooke was waiting for us in room one. I'm sure Carl had his reasons for putting her there. I hoped it wasn't because of their value differences regarding faith choices. I needn't have worried about that. We were in trouble before we sat down.

Brooke jumped to her feet the minute the door opened, crossing her arms in defiance, all five feet eight inches, one hundred twenty pounds of her. Short cropped auburn hair rested just above her ears. She sported three pierced rings in each. I didn't want to think about where else she was pierced.

Carl motioned for her to sit.

Narrowing her green eyes at him, she spat, "After you."

Carl's body tensed. Not a good start. I stepped in front of him. "Well, thank you very much. How thoughtful."

Her intent to get a rise out of us now a failed attempt, she plopped back down into her chair.

"Brooke, my name is Lynzee Rose. This is Detective Carl Watson. Your name is Brooke Rivers, correct? Is that your given name?"

"It's my legal name." She folded her arms across her chest preparing for a fight.

I noted her distinction. "Let me start by saying how sorry I am for your loss. I understand you and Jake were in a relationship together, is that true?"

"Were," she emphasized. "We broke up during Yule."

"You are Wiccan and he a Christian. Was the difference in beliefs the reason you broke up?"

Not prepared to defend her faith with us, her response was slow to come. "Yes. I suppose it came down to that," not offering any more the topic.

I pushed on. "We're talking to Jake's family and friends," I smiled at her, "hoping to track down his last known whereabouts to figure out what happened and when. I'm sure you want closure just as much as we do."

She nodded warily.

"With that end in mind, when did you last see or speak with Jake?"

She hesitated then said, "He called me from his dad's on the twenty-fourth. They had a Christmas Eve morning thing together. He wanted me to spend Christmas Day with him, but I told him I had too much going on with Yule and wouldn't be able to get away. I never heard from him again."

"That doesn't sound like a breakup to me," Carl interjected.

"He said he would call. He didn't. What would you call it?"

Since I might have come to the same conclusion, I decided to continue this line. "I'd like to understand a little more about the breakup from your perspective, Brooke, if you don't mind. Did your relationship cause a problem with your standing in your coven?" I hit a nerve.

With steam coming out her ears, she fumed, "I assume you heard the worst about me from his loser Army friend already."

"Well, Paul is not one of your fans. That's true. He has his opinion. What's yours?"

"What's true is my coven put positive thoughts in support of

Jake coming over. It's hard on a relationship when both people aren't in the coven. It would have left him out of so many things in my life. When he didn't call, I took it as a message from the Goddess to let it go and move on. I did."

"Do you know if he had any plans to see or talk to anyone during the holiday season?" Carl took out his pencil and note pad.

"No. No idea."

I wanted to bring some closure to her relationship with Jake and said, "Does hearing Jake was likely dead change anything about what the Goddess may have been trying to tell you?"

"I don't know. I'll have to put some energy on it."

Carl shifted uneasily in his chair. I pushed on.

"Did he ever mention anyone he was having difficulty with, on the construction job, from his stint in the Army, or anywhere else in his life?"

"Only that jerk-off friend of his. They had an argument. He wouldn't say what about."

Carl didn't want to her Brooke's feelings about Paul. "Tell me your whereabouts on December 24th."

Her voice shrill and sharp, "Why? I already told you I didn't see Jake."

"Because I asked you the question. If you don't answer it, I have cause to hold you over til you do, Ms. Rivers."

"After talking to Jake, I went with friends for Yule festivities. We set up camp on Skatter Creek."

He pulled out a County map, pushing it in her direction. "Show me where you camped."

She gave him the stink eye, grabbed it, and pointed to a spot turning it in his direction, "Right here."

"That puts you around Capitol State Forest. You aware Jake's body turned up at Mima Mounds?"

"I know where the Mounds are if that is what you're asking. You're trying to trick me into saying I knew he was dead which isn't true. The press conference is the first I heard of it."

I had been sitting wondering why Carl didn't pursue Paul's and her relationship. He must have a reason. I said, "Brooke, Jake had been a part of your life once. Our sole purpose is to find out what happened to him and bring his killer to justice. Being uncooperative raises questions for us about your relationship." Leaning into the center of the table, making my message even clearer, "Look at it from our perspective. You had opportunity and motive."

She blinked hard. "How did he die?"

I started to open my mouth in response but Carl stepped in, "We were hoping you could shed some light on that."

"Well, I can't."

"In a related matter to this case, tell us your whereabouts on Tuesday afternoon and evening."

In a voice full of hostility, "Tuesday, I drove around running errands. Wait. Why are you asking me about Tuesday?"

"So, no alibi then," Carl jotted in his notebook.

"I don't need an alibi," she dragged out slowly.

Carl leaned forward, "Right now, you are the last person to see or talk to Jake. Let's not forget, nothing places Jake alive after Christmas Eve. You had contact with him then. In your own words, you thought he'd dumped you. Here's what I think happened. You didn't like it. You, or you and your group, took action." He sat up straight, crossing his arms. "We happen to have video of someone looking an awful lot like you entering and leaving the morgue Tuesday. You have some reason for being there?"

"You think I need to come to a morgue for kicks 'cause I'm a witch, you small-minded bastard?" She stood, pointing hard at Carl as she spoke.

"What I think comes from the information you provided my officer in your statement earlier today." Carl flipped through the pages. "You are a nurse at Providence St. Peter." He laid down the statement and looked at her. "That gives you all kinds of access to people, places, and things." Pointing back but at her chair, he calmed himself down and told her, "Sit down, please."

Brooke appeared to be putting the pieces together about her situation. She stood there contemplating what her next move should be.

Carl reminded her, "A bit more cooperation would be appreciated, or I'm going to think you are impeding our investigation rather than assisting it. Are we clear?"

Brooke sat down but said nothing. Her face showed nothing. The room stayed quiet. I was nervous about what to say or do next. Then, she spoke.

"I'm a nurse. I don't see patients in a morgue, and I don't put them there. It wasn't me. If you knew anything about Wicca, you would know. . ."

Finishing it for her, I said, "You do no harm. We know. I'm sure you'd agree that people do all kinds of things outside their personnel belief system or faith practices. You had opportunity and a motive. You believed Jake broke up with you. Of course, we don't know that he did break up with you, correct? We'll never know."

"No. I'll never know," she said in a hushed voice.

Carl stated his request again. "We do need witnesses to verify your whereabouts from December 24th through the end of December."

"I can't account for every minute that long ago. No one could. When I'm not working my shifts at the hospital, I'm either with other people or I'm alone. If you can't be more specific about dates and times, neither can I."

She clearly did not like Carl, or at best, she did not like his approach with her. It didn't stop him. Glancing at her file, he said, "We'll verify what we can with your employer, Ms. Rivers. But if you can't provide names of persons you spent time with outside of work to corroborate your whereabouts, we can't eliminate you as a suspect."

"You say I had motive. I didn't. We barely knew each other. And Yule is as much about birth as Christmas is. Winter Solstice is a time of feasting and celebration of life, not death."

Carl had had enough of her using Yule and Christmas in the same sentence.

I asked, "Tell me, do you use herbs in your coven's rituals? Do you ever use ground ivy?"

She now eyed me warily. "We burn a variety of ground or cut roots and herbs to promote blessings or to keep out negativity."

"And ground ivy?" Carl asked.

"It's used for abundance and growth. To expand the consciousness. Perhaps you'd be interested, Detective? I know a good herbalist I could recommend," she said smugly.

"Why don't you," pushing a piece of paper and pen in her direction, "write that name and number down for me, if you would."

Eyeing him suspiciously, she did as he asked then pushed both back to him.

This had turned into an interrogation. I was not happy. I decided to try another tack: draw on her helping, professional, side. "Brooke, maybe you can help us. Jake consumed ground ivy sometime before he died. Do you know if he was seeing an herbalist?" I hoped I hadn't overstepped any boundaries.

Carl said nothing; a good sign I hoped.

She relaxed her shoulders and adjusted her position to sit more comfortably in her chair. "No. Jake would never do that. The only herbs he consumed were in his beer."

"Tell me more about that. We understand he was interested in making beer, was that a common interest you two shared?"

"He said he knew a guy who made his own beer. I thought it would be fun to do. That's all. It never happened."

"I'll be the first to admit I don't know a lot about pagan practices. I know December has a lot going on for both Wiccans and Christians."

Her eyes darted back and forth between us as she tried to figure out where this topic was going.

Are you still interested in helping us?" I knew she hadn't actually said she was, but I thought she might want to take my lead.

"Of course I want to help."

"Good. If Jake took part in pagan rituals involving ground ivy, it might help us to understand a little more about them. Say for instance Waning Moon Magic, what's involved in that one?"

Brooke raised an eyebrow. "Jake wouldn't include it in his holiday plans."

"Why's that? If he'd been with you during Yule, he might have wanted to please you?"

"He was Christian. The ceremony is about removing impurities. He would turn to prayer."

"Okay, what about Oak Moon? Did you have a ceremony around this event?"

"I did not take part in any ritual resulting in power over Jake. Nor he over me. It's an involved subject. It's not a factor."

"Okay. Any ceremony where Jake and ground ivy were a featured part?"

"My coven was not involved with Jake other than to put out positive thoughts into the universe for his acceptance of us and our world. That's all there is to say about that."

Carl was not through with her yet. "I understand your husband, Mark, died last year under rather unpleasant circumstances."

Ouch. Brooke was really caught off guard now.

She blinked, swallowed hard, and said, "Leave him out of this."

Carl continued, "If I can, I will, but he was in the Army, like Jake. Were they in the same unit? They know each other or work together? I assure you I wouldn't go down this path if I didn't have to."

"They were in the same unit, yes. No, they didn't work together; They may have known each other in Iraq, I don't know. My husband was a medic. Jake a truck driver."

She opened that door, so I asked, "Is it possible some of your husband's friends might have wanted to avenge his death by killing your boyfriend?"

Brooke was becoming angry with us again. "Do you know

how many suicides occur at Ft. Lewis-McChord base every year? I'm sure you don't. In any case there was nothing to avenge. Jake and I didn't start seeing each other until after my husband died."

Carl went through the open door with me. "When did you start seeing each other?"

"After the funeral. Are we done here?"

There was a lot more we could ask, but she wasn't a suspect, yet, and this was bordering on cruel, in my mind. We sat watching her for a long moment before Carl spoke. "We'll close this interview for now. Until we meet again, then."

Carl stood up. I waited to see what Brooke was going to do.

Brooke studied us for a moment, realized she was being released, and stood up. We all started for the door when Carl stopped her saying, "Oh, and Brooke, don't leave town."

"You need help." She brushed by him and quickened her pace to the elevator.

*　　　*　　　*

Back in Carl's office, I thumbed through Brooke's file admiring the procedure Carl utilized for homicide investigations: a three-step process.

In the first step, information is obtained directly from a witness, or a suspect, about themselves and their relationship to a victim.

Next, follow-up calls clarify, dispute, or expand on the information given by the time we get to the interview room.

Then, the last round verifies or disputes statements from the interview.

"Brooke spent several years in England," I said to Carl leafing through her two-step completed file. "Her parents live in Hastings. And, as you may have guessed, she was born Brooke Anderson, not Rivers."

"Okay. You see anything else useful in there?"

"Here's a surprise. She comes from a military family. Odd she didn't have much to say about that aspect of her life, let alone Jake's, or her husband's."

"Much as I'd like to be rid of her, we may have to talk to her again."

I set down the file trying to place something I couldn't quite wrap my head around.

Carl watched me then asked, "Something on your mind?"

"Can't put my finger on it." I shook my head, trying to shake loose the cobwebs. No luck. "Says here she lives in Tumwater. Wonder if she knows Ranger Dan?"

Carl took the file and made a note. He stuck his head out the door calling out in one motion, "Bill, see if there's a connection between Dan Freis and Brooke Rivers. They both live in Tumwater. Check under the name '*Brooke Anderson*', too. Thanks." He rubbed his eyes and face with his hands as he stood by the door.

"We done for today?"

"Yeah, Lynz. It's been a full day. I'm feeling it. You?"

"I could use a break. Tomorrow?"

"Meet me over at Hawks Diner, eight o'clock. I made arrangements to speak with the hotel manager there."

Then it came to me. That something that had been gnawing at me since we'd ended the interview.

"Brooke wasn't limping."

Carl turned his head quizzically waiting for me to explain myself.

"The person on the security feed entering and leaving the morgue, remember?"

"Ah. Yes. Though, she is a nurse and very capable of ministering to her own injury."

"Keeping her on your white board, then?"

"I'm thinkin' she's with us til the case closes." Carl grabbed the file and dropped it on his desk.

*   *   *

It felt safe to be home. Time for rejuvenation. I changed into my paint and clothes and walked out to the cabin for some family time. I pulled out the large metal toolbox containing dad's carpenter tools from under my workbench. I'd set it aside many times, opting for cleaner jobs. I opened the lid, and gently, like a beautifully wrapped Christmas present, ran my fingers over the contents. Everything inside the box, heavily coated in rust. Some serious time and effort will have to go into restoring these properly. The moment was not to be. Hearing the ringtone assigned to Carl, I answered the call before it went to voicemail.

"Yes?"

"You don't say hello?"

"Carl, give me a break. I didn't have to answer it at all, you know." Realizing this was a less than professional response, I backtracked quickly adding, "I'm sorry. I was in the middle of something. Let me start again. Hello. What's up?"

"Called to update you on alibis, figured I'd be in trouble if I didn't."

He waited for some quick comeback, but I was too tired to play. He continued.

"Paul has an alibi for when the body was taken from the morgue but he doesn't have one for December twenty-fourth. He didn't fly out til Christmas Day. Dan, just the opposite. No alibi to confirm he was at the Preserve during the timeframe the body was taken, but his story checks out for the holidays. He was in Bend."

Still feeling like a jerk, I softened my tone even more. "Unless they worked it together, are they in the clear for the murder?"

"Not altogether. They move down the list. But without an exact date and time of death to work with, I can't remove them altogether. And, we're still looking into whether or not they know each other. There's no obvious connection."

"Why didn't we just ask them if they knew each other?"

"It's all about having the advantage when, or if, it moves from an interview to an interrogation."

Okay. That made sense. I asked, "We pretty much have Jake's death down to the last week of December, right?"

"Last contact he had with anyone we know of was around Christmas and Doc says November or December, so we'll focus on that week til we know different."

"The murderer may not be someone who knew him well enough to lure him out that way. It could have happened anywhere by anyone. We could be way off base." My own feelings of frustration case crept back into my voice.

Carl was not discouraged by my mood and reminded me, "Most of the time, a murder is committed by someone known to the victim. Until we've exhausted that supply, we are on the right path."

"Sorry I sound so negative, Carl."

He continued. "No connection between Brooke and Dan we can find. Tumwater has hundreds of apartment complexes with hundreds of units in each of them. We know they don't live in the same complex. That's all we're going to know unless we start canvassing all of Tumwater. Hope it doesn't come to that."

"Me, too. It was a long shot. How about the coven. Is it possible Dan is a part of it?"

"I doubt it. Checked him out through the Bend area Sheriff. Harmless, good people, he said. Known the kid for ages. They're a Mormon family. I'm thinking if there was anything on the dark side in Dan's life, the Sheriff would know about it."

"I'm stuck on how the killer ended up in the preserve unnoticed."

"Yeah. Me, too. Talked to Dan's supervisor and got the contact info for the previous Ranger. We'll bring him in and ask him about access during his time."

"Anything else on Brooke?"

"Not til tomorrow. There's a lot to check. We'll talk to her again when I can punch a hole in her story. Anyway, wanted to keep you in the loop."

"Thanks, Carl. Good night."

I checked the clock. Past time for dinner. I locked up the cabin hoping I'd be back to my tool restoration project soon.

As I brought water to a boil on the stove, I poured a glass of wine. Minutes later, I had a favorite pasta dish: three-Pepper Pasta. I eat a lot of comfort food in the winter months, when keeping warm is on my mind. It was a good batch. Browned butter, red pepper flakes, black pepper, and pepperocini. A heavy handed toss of grated Asiago cheese topped it off. I opted out of a salad. Pepperocini was vegetable enough for tonight.

Crossing my fingers, I channel surfed til Detective Goren appeared on a favorite repeat. Pasta, wine, and Bobby. A perfect three. He was talking with a shrink; one he was ordered to see.

He questioned her about the focus she put on his hypersensitive state of being. He asked her to explain how his being in continuous motion was not the result of living in the moment, rather than her assessment that he was escaping the here and now. The psychiatrist blinked. They always do for Bobby.

I turned it off. He'd made his point. Boxes don't work for people, only things. Bobby lived life on his own terms. That meant being a loner. It worked for him. I poured another glass of wine and asked myself, '*I'm sensitive. I can overreact, but am I alone because I want to be or have to be?*' No answer.

Exhausted from the day, I rinsed dishes and cookware, and then called it a night. I climbed under the covers and closed my eyes, my mind continued racing between reliving the interviews from earlier today and wondering about the choices I'd made in my life. I tortured myself through a hard night's sleep without any answers to the case or my own situation.

CHAPTER 7

"Bad night?" Carl watched me approach the table.

"Yeah, something I watched on TV last night didn't sit well. Kinda stayed with me. I'm okay." I don't think he bought it, but he let it go. I ordered a bacon cheese omelet and sat back with my first cup of coffee of the day. I left the house fast, not stopping to make my usual brew. "Carl, let's try someplace new for breakfast. I think we're in a rut."

"Sure, no problem."

"Speaking of ruts, we're into this investigation a full week. We're still at the starting line. Do you see an end in sight?" I came off sounding edgy, to put it nicely, but it was too late to take it back.

Carl eyed me for a moment then answered, "I thought we were in a bit of a dead end til the bones were taken. Then, I changed my mind."

Still regretting showing my melancholy side, I tried to explain. "You know, we've not worked a case like this one before. It doesn't feel like a random act. Nor does it seem like a one-to-one kind of crime to me."

"I'm not sure what that means, Lynz. But, I think we're closer to catching the killer than you think."

I started to question him more, but breakfast arrived. Perhaps food would tame my mood. Besides, who knew how the day would turn out. It might be our only sit down of the day, if yesterday was any example.

We finished eating and sat back, full and content, even me.

Carl said, "I scheduled our interview with the hotel manager here since he's right next door. I'm happy to try a different place for breakfast. I admit I can be a 'in a rut' kinda guy."

"I really don't see you that way. I'm sorry if it came out like that."

Carl closed the subject saying, "He's bringing copies of employment files for the crew that did the Inn project. Ground zero for Jake's brief construction career."

We settled into another cup of coffee. The hostess at the front of the restaurant started chatting with a man in a stylish grey suit and burgundy tie. She pointed to our table. Nodding, he walked our way. Carl turned in the direction I was looking, and then rose to greet our guest. "I'm Detective Carl Watson and this is Lynzee Rose."

"Hi, I'm Craig Monroe," extending his hand with a polished smile. He pulled out a chair and sat down. "I understand you want information about the construction employees for our hotel here in Lacey. It's a rather an unusual request. May I ask why you want them?"

"As you probably heard on the news, we found a young man's body, a homicide victim, who turns out to have been one of your employees, Jake Mathews. Appears he died sometime in December."

"Yes, I heard about that. I didn't know him personally. I manage new hotel startups in the Western jurisdiction. I don't involve myself directly with the crews. The project site manager supervises our construction employees. We hire locally, for the most part. A few, like Jake, who prove themselves, are invited to stay on and travel with us to other hotel construction projects."

"So, Jake was one of those employees?" I asked to confirm what he said.

"Yes. However, he would have been off the clock in December."

"How's that?"

"The Lacey project finished up late November and the Texas location he was due to report at didn't start til late December. Our project manager stays on payroll year round, one of the few that do." He flipped through his files and moved one of them to the top. "I moved Jake's file to the top for you. Our crew supervisor and project manager is Scott Connors. Been with us about four years."

"Where is he now?"

"He finished his work at our Houston Inn late April. He's in Oregon setting up for our next project. Very responsible. The crews seem to like working with him."

Craig pulled an envelope from the inside pocket of his suit jacket and stood up. "I've prepared a letter giving Scott permission to answer your questions about the crew that worked this project. His contact information is in the letter. I took the liberty of faxing him a copy, as well."

Carl stood up and took the letter. He bristled as he read it. Putting it back into the envelope, he said. "Thank you." His facial expression was not on par with his words. "Our investigation may include talking to individual members of the work crew on our own. The intent of this letter is appreciated, Mr. Monroe, but our investigation will lead where it leads, including talking to people with or without your permission, and when and where we choose."

"I understand, Detective. I ask only that your inquiries be handled discreetly where possible. I'd like to be able to put an end to this matter quickly. I am certain your inquiry will end with our reputation intact. Our company prides itself on our hiring process and business practices. We don't employee criminals." He pushed the files toward Carl, nodded to both of us, got up from the table, turned, and left the restaurant.

Carl grabbed them and told me, "Breakfast is on me. I'm thinking this meal isn't going to sit all that well."

"Okay. But the next one's on me," I insisted. "To your office?"

"Yep. I'll ask Bill to arrange for us to meet with Scott. I wish Mr. Monroe hadn't alerted his project manager already.

"Well, he sounds like management. The hotel probably has different rules for talking to management personnel."

"Still. We're stuck with the situation now. "Tom will take statements from the rest of the crew. We may or may not need to meet with them. See you back at the office."

*　　　*　　　*

When I arrived, Carl was studying his white board. The names *'Brooke, Paul, Dan, Scott, Joe'* were written in black. A red line separated the columns of names. Another column was marked, *'Jake'*, in green marker, down mid way under Jake's name, and enclosed in parenthesis he wrote, *'Mark'*. He stood staring hard, his face resting in one hand, his body in an at ease position. Turning toward me, he said, "Scott's voicemail says he's on holiday til Tuesday. Bill left a message asking him to call us ASAP."

I pointed to the white board and the assortment of colored markers. "Okay. What are you doing there?"

"I think it's time we put the pieces we do have together here on the board," he tipped his head forward as he spoke. "See if we can make any connections or draw some conclusions. I've left space to add the names of other persons of interest as they develop."

"I see."

"We have the girlfriend, the best friend, the person who discovered the body, the boss, and the family member. The usual array of suspects."

I picked up the case file he had on top, Jake Mathews. "Okay, says he was a Christian. Born Jacob Mathews." He wrote as I talked. "No church listed. Brooke is his girlfriend, but his status is single. Paul's his best friend. Joe is his dad. I'm not seeing any other family here. We now know that Jake worked for Scott. No known enemies. No arrests. A clean kid leading a normal life."

Carl wrote *'December 24'* in the Jake column and underlined it twice and emphasized it by say, "And this is the date anyone last had contact with him."

We went through all the files then stepped back to look at what we had.

Carl slapped at the board. "Dang. I want Scott in here now. Wonder if I could push Mr. Monroe into ordering him to back here from Oregon."

"I think as an employer, Mr. Monroe would have to pay Scott, his employee, holiday pay, time and a half at the least. to order him here to talk to us in person. Don't count on it. You do remember we are entering Memorial Day weekend as we speak, don't you?"

"Yeah. I remember. And if Monroe was gonna have to put money anywhere other than on his *'Eye-tal-yun'* suits, he wouldn't be happy about it."

I was about to ask Carl if he had any plans for the weekend when Tom came in with a light knock on the door. Perhaps for the best.

Tom said, "We didn't get much from calling the construction employees. One guy remembers Jake talking about making beer, but that's all. They preferred Budweiser, so they didn't have much to talk about. The crew consisted of five regulars, all from the Olympia area. All of them liked the work and would work for the hotel again if asked."

"That's the whole crew?" Carl asked.

"Two additional guys from Labor Ready joined them as needed. Scott supervised the whole bunch. A few of them agreed to come down and give formal statements for their whereabouts on December twenty-fourth. The others said they wanted to talk to a lawyer first. We may want to include contacting the hotel's list of subcontractors if this turns into a dead end."

"Thanks, Tom. Set that stuff on the table. I'll get back to you about subcontractors once I see how cooperative Mr. Craig Monroe is going to be."

"One more thing," Tom tipped his head toward our whiteboard, "Scott is Ralph Connors' son."

I let out a whistle. "Now, that's interesting."

"*It's a small world after all*," Carl chimed in a singsong voice while picking up his marker. "What do we have on Scott?"

Carl added Ralph's name next to Scott's. His theory of this murder more evident the further we progressed. His top suspects were either family members, friends, Brooke and Paul. Ranger Dan came in a close third since he discovered the body.

"Carl, I think adding Ralph to your list of suspects is a reach. I don't see a motive for him or any connection to him and Jake."

"True. Since we are looking at his son, who worked with Jake, I'll keep him on the board all the same."

I read Tom's research details to him. "Scott's listed as single. Six feet tall, one hundred eighty pounds. Thirty-five years old. Blue eyes. Brown hair. Parents are Ralph and Gretchen Connors. No sisters or brothers. Permanent address listed as the farm in Littlerock. College graduate from Western Washington University. Been with the hotel chain four years. Before that, he worked as an architect for a Seattle firm. Looks like that's how he made his connection with his current employer."

I noticed Tom was still with us, studying the list.

Carl noticed, too. "Do you have any news about bringing in the previous Ranger for us to talk to today?"

"Yes, sir. He'll be in room three at eleven." Tom left as the phone on Carl's desk started ringing.

I stood up and added '*microbrew/beer making?*' under Jake's name. I put parenthesis around Ralph's name. I was putting my own mark and objection to it being there. I added '*special ops/army?*' to the list of column names. I thought we needed to explore that group further, certainly, before we started poking into poor Ralph's life.

Carl hung up and came back around his desk to the board.

I looked over at him and said, "I wonder if Scott's the beer maker we heard about," pointing at the board then adding the same notation I'd put under Jake's name. I tipped my head toward the phone waiting for him to brief me.

"Oh, that was the store manager in Littlerock. He went through his records, didn't find any for a load of dirt sold in either November or December. I don't think it would do us any good to go back further right now, unless we get a viable suspect or really desperate."

"Yeah, that would have been too easy. FYI, I'm going to head down to the Mounds tomorrow. I'll check in on how Ranger Dan's dirt removal project is progressing and stop and talk to Ralph some more if that's okay."

"So, you're on billable time then?"

"Does it only count when we're together?"

"No, no. I didn't mean that at all. This contracting business is tricky when it comes to murder investigations. I need to know for the bean counters."

"Ah, that makes sense."

He shuffled his feet thinking how to say it, and then just did. "And, you have to have a deputy with you at all times. Investigations and interviews have to include one of our officers. I'll let them know you're coming down in the morning."

"Sure, I understand. I'll stay with a member of your team at all times."

"About Ralph. Hold off talking to him for now. I want a chance to talk with his son before we talk to Ralph about that relationship."

"I would like to check on him, would that be okay?"

"Sure, that's fine as long as you take a detective with you and keep it light. No mention of us trying to get in touch with Scott. I'd like to go with you, but I'm locked into some other things Saturday and Sunday."

That answered my previous thought about spending time together over the holiday weekend. I said, "I'll be fine. Mostly going down for another look from a different perspective, a new view of it. Like you did with this chart you've made," pointing at the white board.

"How do you mean?"

We had a half hour until our scheduled interview with the retired Mima Mounds Ranger. I had enough time to explain it.

"One of my favorite mediations has helped me many times when things don't look right or are not as they seem. I'll give you the short version." I sat down and motioned for Carl to sit across from me.

"Two people arrive at my office. We all take a seat at the table. First, an upwardly mobile executive tells his story of how trees belonging to his downhill neighbor were unsightly and ruining the expansive view for which he had paid a bundle. He had offered to pay to have them cut down. His neighbor said no. He brings out pictures of the trees as proof to their unkempt and overgrown condition.

Next, the neighbor, an older woman tells her story of how the trees provide shade in the summer and protection from winter's harsh elements. She says her late husband planted them over thirty-five years ago and cared for them right up to the day he died five years ago. She insists her trees are not the same trees her neighbor is discussing. She, too, has pictures.

The pictures are passed between them, and much to their dismay, neither recognizes the trees in the other's photos. The more they try to make a match of them to prove their points, the more it becomes clear it can't be done.

I pick up each set of photos and look through them. One set shows charming fairytale book trees and the other set show trees reminding me of any number of scary movies I'd seen."

"What happened?"

"I asked them to return home and arrange a visit to each other's property to see the trees from each other's homes. The elderly woman was to view the trees from her neighbor's house using his pictures. The exec is to go to her home and look at her trees using her pictures. I ask them to come back in two days to meet with me again."

"This reminds me of an old biblical character. . ."

"King Solomon?"

"Yeah. How do you know about him?"

"Well, I may not go to church, but I happen to know a lot about him. He's a long time favorite. A big reason I went into mediation, if you must know." That, I thought, and the fact I could remain in relationship neutrality mode and paid to do so. No need to share that second part. "So, do you want to know how it ends or not?" I teased.

"I do."

"Two days later, they return to the table. In fact, they rode together. They reached a solution themselves, my work was done."

"How so?"

"Once they saw the trees from each other's perspective, they understood each other's point of view. The issue for both of them was the trees. To one, it was a positive life factor. To the other, a negative."

"Okay. I get that now."

"The interests for each were different, which is what brought them to me. The interest for the uphill neighbor was an unrestricted view. The interest for our widow was shade and protection. The successful conclusion to this story is both were winners, the two shared the cost to have the trees topped professionally, restoring his view, without destroying the trees. The widow kept the shade and security the lower half of the trees provided. And, she kept what mattered most-- the connection to her husband."

"Did you make up that story?"

"No way. It happened just the way I told it." I put my hand up and went through the motion of swearing on a stack of Bibles.

Carl looked at me intently, perhaps waiting for me to be struck by lightning. Then again, maybe it was because one of my heroes is King Solomon. He continued his stare. "And how do you apply that to our current situation?"

"Elementary, Watson. What we have is Mima Mounds," I said rising and pointing to the whiteboard. "What we need is to put the 'pictures' together," picking up and dropping the files on the table for affect, "and go back to the trees, the Mounds in our case, for another look."

"So, are you're saying the issue for the killer and for us is the same?"

"Not us. The issue for the killer is the Mima Mounds field. For Jake, the issue is the Mounds only if that is why he went there, or that he went there willingly; that is, alive. In any case, the issue that brought them together, that infamous night, is the same issue. We just don't know what it was. We, just like in my mediation story, sort out the interests, or reasons, that brought the two together. I got up and found some empty space on Carl's white board. I wrote: *Mima Mounds: above ground mound. Made to fit with other mounds.* . Then, I wrote: *Killer: Buried victim alive. Buried victim fully dressed. Buried victim in December. Incapacitated victim with paralyzing wound to neck.* Then, next to Jake's name, I wrote: *'Male. Healthy. Single. Veteran. Young. Only child. Good looking. Construction Worker.*

The clock ran out. I put the marker down with a *'to be continued'* glance to Carl.

We hurried off to the interview room. Tom met us with file in hand. He was about to leave when Carl stopped him.

"Tom, why don't you join us on this one."

Tom's dark eyes lit up. "Sure. If you think I can be of use."

"You are already of major benefit to these cases with what you do. I'm thinking we need to build your resume up some."

Tom beamed and said, "After you." Opening the door, he ushered us into the room. Tom made the introductions. "Mr. Baker, this is Detective Carl Watson and our case consultant, Lynzee Rose." He turned to Carl and me, pointing out two seats at the table, while he took a third. "We won't take up too much of your day. Just a few questions about security at the Preserve during the time you were Ranger compared to how things are being done today."

Mr. Baker was hovering in his late sixties, well on his way to his seventies, in decent shape for having had a recent heart attack. I made a mental note to check on Joe. I read his eagerness as someone more interested in getting the lowdown on what went down at the Mounds than offering a whole lot of useful information to the investigation. But, when you're grasping at straws, you drink from any glass. I put my preconceived notion of our guest aside.

"Sure. Sure. Call me Gare. Anything I can do to help. I know those little hills real well. Made a career out of 'em right when the park was established all the way up to this season," he chuckled to himself. "Darnedest thing. Heard it on the news. Finding a body out there. What's next in this world?" Shaking his head, "I'm sure this thing's going to bring out those alien busters again."

Say what? I thought better of it, but said it anyway, "Aliens?" A promising theory on the Mounds I'd been pondering since this case began a week ago rolled forward in my mind.

"Yeah, weirdoes driving an old Airstream. They make their way across the country tryin' to prove their theory about mound fields being part of an alien invasion. Call themselves 'Alien Mound Invasion Detectors, AMID'. Said the name is to remind us we have aliens 'AMID' us." He chuckled again. "Every couple a years they make their way back to our little corner of mounds. Let me think now." He stroked his graying whiskers with a cigarette stained hand, "Yeah, they were here a year ago. Shouldn't have to see them again for another season, I hope."

Deciding not to indulge me any further, Carl brought us back down to earth. "I'm more interested in access to the Mounds, if you don't mind," looking in my direction.

Tom covered his mouth with one hand to keep from smiling aloud.

Thinking I'd save this discussion with Ranger Gare til a more private time, I asked instead, "Has the entrance gate always had a lock?"

"Not always. But like I said, we had folks, alien chasers included, that didn't follow our seasonal schedule. It's a day use facility, but people tried bringing in RVs, usin' the place as a free campground, which it isn't," he emphasized. "Had our share of late night parties goin' on out in the fields, too. Putting a locked gate across the entrance took care of all three problems: campers, partiers, and kooks."

I shifted uncomfortably hoping to keep from being thrown into his '*kooks*' category.

Tom asked, "Were the locks changed when you retired?"

"Not that I heard. I still got my key," smiling as he pulled his key ring out of his pocket showing us the gate key.

Tom tried tiptoeing around this point. "How many copies do you suppose are out there?"

"Well, I don't want to find myself in a heap of trouble having this keys so's it affects my retirement…"

Leaning forward with assurance in his voice, Tom said, "We're not going to report it. We'll leave the return of the key to you. What we do need is an understanding of how many people *might* have a key making it possible to drive into the Mounds when they wanted."

"Oh, well, that what happened? Hmmm, you'd have to have a key alright or know where the back entrance is."

We all sat up straight.

"Another entrance?" Carl was first out of the proverbial gate.

He jerked back at our sudden group movement, then relaxed and said, "We had a section of fence hinged for when we needed to drive into the back half of the Mounds without rolling over the first half. No lock on it. Didn't have need to back then. It was secluded and, if you didn't know where it was, you would have a hard time trying to find it. But, now with these shenanigans and all, probably should rethink that and put a lock on it."

Tom whipped out a map of the area.

"Would you point out the location of that fence for me, sir?"

Pulling out a set of double strength reading glasses, Gare flipped the map around from end to end til he found what he was looking for." Right here, along the north edge."

Carl stood up for a better view of the location.

Tom drew a circle of the location on the map.

I decided tomorrow's schedule would include a look at this north gate.

Former Ranger Baker, pleased with being useful to our investigation, explained the gate situation further. "Course, there's no need to drive onto the Mounds from there anymore. We used it to clear out storm debris, and there's less of that every year. What's down is down already. That fence section is probably all overgrown by now; hasn't been used in years." He thought for a minute and then added, "As far as keys to the main gate, there's mine, the one the new Ranger has, the Supervisor has one, and I don't know who else would have need of one. But, thinking about it now, I did keep an extra hanging in the office for emergencies. Sometimes, I'd forget mine at home," he looked at us apologetically. "It's probably still hanging there."

Hmmm, I thought. I should check on that, too.

"You've been a big help to this investigation, Mr. Baker. If you think of anything else, please don't hesitate to give us a call," Carl rose to his feet.

Tom followed.

Gare wasn't through with me. He leaned forward and said in a hushed voice, "We got a lot of history and mystery down in the Littlerock mounds. I know the story about these mounds being formed in 9,000 BC due to the retreat of the glaciers in the area. But, that don't explain mounds in Texas, now does it?"

I didn't really know.

He gave me a wink and stood to leave. Coming around the table, he shook my hand with a parting word. "Gophers. Glaciers. Earthquakes. Volcanoes. Aliens. Tsunamis. Ancient Fish Nests. Wind Erosion. Steam Vents. I've heard 'em all."

He had my attention. I stood up but found I didn't know what to say to all that.

He didn't wait for me. He had something else in mind. "You take a good hard look at an aerial view of 'em sometime. If they don't look like God's tear drops, then I don't know what does."

With that, he said his goodbyes.

I escorted him to the elevator.

Tom went back to his desk to contact Ranger Dan about extra gate keys.

I walked back to the office on autopilot, wondering what the remark about tear shaped mounds meant.

Already at his desk, Carl was on the phone instructing his duty officers at the Mounds on where to locate the old gate access panel. He described the section from the map suggesting they include Ranger Dan to help find it. By the time he finished with the call, Tom returned with a key count.

"Ranger has a key. There's a spare hanging in the office." He turned to go and then remembering, "Oh. He said to tell you unloading a truck load of dirt can be done in a half hour tops." Tom gave a salute saying he was off for a quick lunch.

I sat looking at the whiteboard wondering what to do with it next. I did the math. "Half hour dumping the dirt, another hour to get the body positioned, buried, and the mound sculpted. This took well thought out time. Carl, it had to be done Christmas Eve, Christmas Day, or the day after. Perhaps as late as December thirtieth or thirty-first."

"Why those days?"

"Those are days when people are preoccupied with holiday stuff and would not be paying attention to what might be going on in the Mounds."

Writing down, *'remains taken'* in a new column, Carl stared at the list of entries we'd made to the board today.

Turning toward me, he said, "I think you're right. No sense of urgency or panic in finishing the work. He or she wanted it done right." He picked up a pink message slip from his desk and read it. Walking back to the whiteboard, he drew an orange asterisk next to Paul's name.

"Paul's in the clear?"

"We verified he was with a study partner when the remains were taken. And, on the twenty-fourth, he spent the night at a motel near the airport." He stared at the board then said, "I see you added a new suspect to my list?"

"The wound on Jake's neck is eating at me in terms of suspects. It's a red flag. We don't have anyone but Paul's name on our list, but that business between Jake and Brooke tells me someone from his Army unit may have not liked it one bit. Enough to do something about it."

Carl tapped his index finger at the 'special ops/army' entry a couple of times then said, "Let's have a meet-up with the base commander. See what we can learn about Jake's unit including their work over in Iraq."

"Good. Anything check out on Brooke's statements?"

"No alibi yet. I'd like to believe Jake's dad isn't involved, but he doesn't alibi out either."

"That's silly. There's no way he should be on that list of yours," I challenged.

"Ralph Connors is still on the list, too. I know that doesn't make you any too happy, either." Spotting my parenthetic addition, he offered by way of explanation, "I know our list seems all over the place. But, ninety percent of the time during the holidays, it's family or friends involved in crimes against other persons. No one more than me wishes that weren't true." Carl took the orange marker and wrote in big letters below the list of names, 'MOTIVE?'

"Well, then, if the only motive you're sure about is holiday drama, we have Joe and Brooke as our primary suspects. I'll bet you a beer on it not being Joe, though."

"I wish I could say the same. The holiday season and the gaps in their communication, combined with the two of them estranged after his mom's death, sends up a red flag for me. Guess that's not part of that new perspective you were talking about," winking to let me know he didn't doze off during my mediation lesson.

"There can be more than one issue in this case. We have Mima Mounds, even beer making. You've come up with third: Christmas holiday."

"I think we have to consider it."

"It's certainly a common subject in each of the interviews we've done so far. Minus Gare, of course. How's Joe doing, by the way?"

"Sheriff says he's going home tomorrow, as long as things go okay for him the rest of today. County lined up home nursing care for a few months. Picking up the cost of his medical bills, whatever his insurance doesn't cover. Cross your fingers and hope he doesn't sue."

*　　　*　　　*

We broke for lunch. My hour dedicated to shopping for the annual Memorial Day weekend Johnson Point Community poker run. Volunteering to be a host stop for this year's event meant one of my errands included the liquor store. Although it is not a requirement, you aren't asked to host a stop again if you didn't bring out booze of some kind. Snack foods are secondary. What was I thinking when I agreed to this? Fifty people pulling up to a screeching halt in golf carts in a race for a winning poker hand.

Hurrying to the elevator, I heard the phone ringing behind me. Glancing back, Carl motioned me to return. Crap.

His one-sided conversation hinted he had Scott Connors on the other end. I worked on my shopping list while he talked. He ended the call. Standing up, he went over to the whiteboard, hands on his trim hips. "As you figured out, that was Scott. Says he's tied up in Oregon til Tuesday morning, camping, already made plans with friends. Says he and Jake talked about micro beers, but he didn't know if Jake ever started making beer. The two of them stopped in at the Spar or Ram for a pint after work occasionally. As far as anyone else Jake hung out with, Brooke and Paul are the only ones he knew about."

"When's the last time he saw or spoke to Jake?"

"December 23rd. He took off for the new hotel construction site in Texas. Expected to see him on site, but he never showed."

"Scott have an alibi for the holidays?"

"Says he clocked in down in Texas day after Christmas. Leaves the twenty-fourth and twenty-fifth unaccounted for. Told him to bring me gas, food, and hotel receipts for those days. I Let him know we are expecting him Tuesday afternoon in my office. I'll have a copy of his work records for last half of December sent over." Carl penned in additional entries to the whiteboard next to Scott's name. "We have a whole lot of people without alibis for the most important family season of the year."

I think his meaning was that a whole lot of people spend them alone. A sad fact of which I know a good deal about. Since I am part of the statistical group, I offered an observation. "Wow. He didn't spend Christmas with his dad. That's sad for Ralph."

Carl left that alone. "Dan did spend a considerable amount of time in Bend this past winter. Covered for the holiday. Home with lots of family around him." He looked up letting me know that just as many people spend time with family as not. Putting a hole in my 'we're all alone' Christmas theory. He went on with the alibi list. "Paul checks out as flying out when he said, so he's covered for Christmas holiday. Brooke? I'm sure she'll be vouched for by her group. Don't look forward to unraveling our way through her mess." He moved back to the white board. "No dirt sold in November or December, if it came from Littlerock. Seems like a long time to be hauling it around if you loaded up in September or October."

Another thought occurred to me. "Construction sites have lots of dirt. Decent topsoil is used or sold."

"Good point. I'll call to our friend Mr. Monroe and ask for a list where the topsoil went. Nice work, Lynz."

I checked my watch. I had to get moving if I had any hope of beating the crowds. "I think I'll call it a day, if that's okay with you?"

"Sure. You mentioned you had shopping to do. Go on. You earned your paycheck today. I'll call if I hear anything. Let me know how it goes tomorrow down at the Mounds." He smiled and waved me out.

I took a shortcut to Ralph's Thriftway to pick up the makings of my snack tray and beverages for Sunday. Making good time, I drove through our entrance gate and noticed Lori, our office manager, was still on the clock. I pulled up next to her car and parked. Hurrying into the small building to grab my mail, I knocked lightly on her private office door.

She peered around to see if anyone else was in the vicinity then swung the door open. "Hey, just finishing up. " What's up?"

"Picked up my supplies for the Poker Run on Sunday afternoon. You still coming to help me?"

"Absolutely. I'll be at your place at two. Do you know where you are on the route?"

"The Activities Manager told me it would be around three."

"Cool. What'd you get?"

"Pink lemonade flavored vodka, not the cheapest brand, but close. Thought we'd mix it with pink lemonade. Make a pitcher of them. I'll make a pitcher without the vodka, too."

"Sounds good. " I have plastic glasses. They're the perfect size. Holds six ounces, so with ice added, they won't be sloshed in the first hour. They still have a long afternoon ahead after they leave your place. Did you load up on ice?"

"I did."

"How about snacks?"

"I had a harder time with that and settled on a fruit platter. Strawberries and honeydew melon. Think that's okay?" I wanted all the chips I could put my hands on, but settled on portraying a healthy image to my guests instead.

"I think it sounds very healthful, she giggled at me. " I'll bring banana bread." Lori's not afraid to talk about food, taboo for those of us with any weight concerns.

"Great. What all do I need to have ready and what happens exactly?"

"Oh, that's right. This is your first hosting. Always plan for rain, it wouldn't be the first time. Have your yard umbrella set up with a small table and two chairs under it for the game officials to sit at. Even if the sun is out, they'll appreciate it. The two officials arrive in the first cart to set up the poker wheel. That goes under the umbrella, too, next to the card table. Players try to cut each other off, or pass each other to be in the front of the line, so stay away from the road until the event is completely over."

"Should I move my car somewhere safe?" I was concerned about property damage now. Why did I decide to do this?

"Naw. It sounds worse than it is. Really. Don't worry. Here's how it works. Players line up, spin the wheel. No need to do chairs for anyone but the two officials. People stay out of the weather sitting in their carts. And, if it's nice, they'll appreciate standing and stretching. Overall, it takes about a half hour at each stop. They eat and drink til everyone is through their turn at the poker wheel, then leave."

"I've heard these can get a bit crazy?"

"You picked the first one of the season, so you won't have any water gun fights. That is messy. And, you're early on the route, so they won't be falling out of their carts yet. You should be fine. Leon's on standby and will make an appearance if things go wild."

"Okay." She picked up the hesitation in my voice.

"Thanks for signing up. Don't worry; I'll be with you to help. It's great to have you be part of our Community events. This activity is only for those with golf carts or who hitch a ride. Course, you can seat four people in some of those. Still, we shouldn't have more than fifty guests from what the registrations tell me. It'll be fun. You'll see."

I left her to finish her work and get home to start her holiday weekend. I hoped this event didn't put me smack dab in the middle of another Sheriff call out. I knew who would smugly take that call, smiling and shaking his head all the way.

Everything refrigerated, with the vodka and pink lemonade in the freezer, my work was done. I didn't want to cook later tonight, so I had stopped to pick up a Papa Murphy's pepperoni pizza to pop in the oven with a side of Alaska Amber. Thin crust DeLITE, cooked to perfection only when the oil from the pepperoni oozes out in little pools. It was the closest I'd found to my fave: Tacoma's Clover Leaf Pizza. Still, when cravings win out over gas prices, I drive the distance.

Our predicted rare three days of sun and no rain didn't rule out Olympia mist, a phenomenon allowing walking from location to location without getting wet. Smiling, I made my way to the cabin thinking about this strange place: weather and community. It was early enough to do some work on dad's tools before dark.

I readied the hose, hanging it off the concrete birdbath I turned into an outdoor sink and secured to a tree stump, now pedestal. With running water and a sink available for my restoration work, it was time to rub the rust off the tools.

Entering the cabin, *'that peaceful easy feeling'* welcomed me inside. Therapeutic time away from the case will help put a fresh eye on it for my trip tomorrow. I thought about what Mr. Baker said, *'Take a good long look at an aerial shot of them sometime, if they don't look like God's tear drops, I don't know what does."* Making a mental note to do just that and call him about it in the morning, I might as well ask him what he knows about the neighbors bordering the Mounds, too. He probably already pegged me as someone who likes hearing the local gossip. I can make use of the stereotype.

My project had been interrupted yesterday. Today, there will be no interruptions. I hoisted up the two-foot long metal toolbox representing dad's part time work. Having completed an extensive research on old tools, I was ready to enhance the experience with my newly acquired information.

The first thing out was dad's carpenter pencil. I held it between my fingers. Stronger than standard hexagonal type, their shape is flat so they don't roll off or blow away. The rectangular lead had to be sharpened with a knife. I pictured my dad doing that.

Next, a metal zigzag ruler, indispensable to carpenters until creation of the self-retracting pocket tape. The fun I used to have playing with it, turning it into assorted shapes. I pulled out screwdrivers, pliers, and a chalk line from the top tray. Other than the rust, they were all in good shape.

Lifting out the top tray, I found an assortment of small and larger tools. A coffin shaped smoothing plane. No connecting memory. It was very rusty. What came next made me catch my breath and drop to my workbench stool. In my hand, I held our murder weapon. Not an ice pick. I ran to the house, grabbed my phone, and speed dialed Carl. He answered on the first ring.

"I know what the murder weapon was. Is. A scratch awl. Not an ice pick. I'm holding it in my hand right now. You better come over."

Taking what seemed like forever, he asked for a coherent distinction. "You mean you have a scratch awl in your hand or you have *the* murder weapon?"

"Sorry. I mean I don't have the murder weapon. I have what was the murder weapon," making it clear as mud.

Carl decided this conversation wasn't going to improve over the phone.

"I'm on my way."

"I'll put the pizza on."

Certain the connection was lost on him, I didn't take time to explain I was just thinking out loud. By the time I closed up the cabin and pre-heated the oven, Carl was buzzing me at the entrance gate.

With mere seconds to straighten up the place and myself, I made it to the door just as he knocked.

Still a bit dazed, I said, "Hey. Come in. Pizza will be out in flash. Beer?"

"Maybe, I better hear the story from the top and see this '*awl*' before I call myself officially off duty."

Point taken. I may have sounded like the kook he hoped I wasn't.

I glanced around as he entered to see his personal car in the drive. The neighbors will appreciate that. Closing the door, I pointed to one of two wingback chairs and handed him the awl. "It wasn't an ice pick. It's a scratch awl." I plopped down exhausted from the adrenalin rush and release of information.

Carl examined the tool with its wood handle and four-inch steel tip. "I think this has definite possibilities. I'll get this to Doc in the morning. He'll have to work off the X-rays and his notes. Best we'll learn is that it is consistent with the wound." He rolled the tool around in his hands. "Only people I know who have one of these are old carpenters."

"That makes sense."

He nodded, and then placed my scratch awl in an evidence bag. He wrote my name in big letters on the outside and added his name to make the point he would take responsibility for returning it to me. Looking up at me with a smile, he said, "Great work, Lynzee. How'd you come by this, if you don't mind me asking?"

"It's a good thing we both know I'm not a suspect, or I'd be concerned by that question, Carl." I laughed. He seemed relieved I'd chosen to laugh and not throw something at him.

"It belonged to my dad. He was a part-time carpenter and full time fisherman."

Relieved and satisfied with my answer, he said, "I'll take that beer, now."

He had no complaints about my pizza or beer selection. In fact, Alaska Amber seemed to be high on his taste bud list. Halfway through the Pizza, he said, "I've got some news, too."

Glad to have the focus off my over exuberant discovery, I looked up. "And that would be?"

Faded blue jeans and a sky blue T-shirt tucked in, he looked good casual. I wondered how I looked to him. Short on time to do more than brush my teeth and hair before he arrived, I decided to refocus on what he was saying and stop worrying about my appearance.

"Mr. Monroe tells me the best grade top soil is put back into the landscaping around the hotels. Any excess is donated to non-profit community service projects. He's pulling records on where the topsoil went and will fax them over. Said he'll send along what he has by way of December time records for Scott after he runs it by his lawyers."

Glancing around as though it was the first time he'd seen the inside, I became self-conscious. Maybe it was the first time. Could that be? Not remembering made me even more uncomfortable and embarrassed. "Let's sit out on the deck and have another beer."

He stood up and went straight to my refrigerator. Grabbing two, he popped the caps, and pointed the way. Before I could react, he sat down outside on one side of my wicker sofa.

I blinked and quickly grabbed the wicker chair so I wouldn't look like I didn't know where to sit. The evening air was cool but pleasant. Suddenly warm, I didn't need the fleece vest I'd grabbed. I felt I needed to explain myself.

"I'm not a nut, Carl. I'm only interested in mound theories as they apply to solving the case."

"I know you're not nuts. I wouldn't be working with you if I thought you were. I'm hoping we'll have a long and successful relationship."

Things were really warming up now, including my armpits.

"Say, as a heads up, this place is having one of their infamous golf cart poker runs Sunday. I'm hoping we won't be seeing you at its conclusion." Nice dodge. Geez.

He raised his eyebrows and leaned his head to one side. My guess? He was remembering our first encounter.

"Ah, yes. The golf cart gang. Our first meeting." He made eye contact but didn't elaborate. Neither did I.

We shared our past case stories, revisiting the missteps along the way and the satisfactions we had shared resolving cases together. This simple exercise was helping me with the frustrations I had been feeling with our current case.

No murder investigation is forgotten. Some people can archive a case from the emotions it wreaks havoc on; not a skill set I own. Allowing myself to pull out a bright spot from the horror helps me maintain my sanity. Carl's visit and our talk did just that. I felt ready for tomorrow.

In bed, listening more than watching, Detective Goren questions a woman's attitude about whether she should have aborted her child rather than bring it into the world. Goren compares her attitude about life and death to the kind one makes in choosing which shoes to wear. My mind drifted off into sleep, and I found myself once again entwined in the enigma of abandonment issues, those that won't allow me to feel wanted by another person.

I can still see the day as if it was yesterday. She came rushing over to my Tacoma house in Old Town announcing she'd written a story, would I read it and tell her what I thought. Mom writing a story came as a shock; she was a fisherman's wife, was there more to her? Knowing she loved to read, roomfuls of books as a testimony, I sat down to read what she'd written in her own hand.

The story began with confessions of an unfulfilled smart and capable woman thrust into a life as a housewife and stay-at-home mom, with three young daughters in her care. No future for herself. The story goes through the years of mounting depression that begins to transfer to paranoid fears for her daughters' futures. Would they face the same empty and unsatisfying life? As the story nears the end, she is watching her daughters at play together in the bathtub. Her concern reached a pinnacle point for the one she called *'Ellie'*. *'Not like the others…fragile, too sensitive'* she wrote. The hairs on my neck stood up. Then I read, *'I should hold her head underwater and save her from the hurt and pain life will surely bring her.'*

Springing to my feet, I had frantically waved the pages in her face, and screeched at her all in one motion, *'How could you? How could you?'* She shouted back in defense, *'It's just a story. It's fiction. It's not true.'*

We both knew differently. The look we shared in that moment said it all. Tears streaming down my face, I searched hers, telling her how as an adult, I had not been able to take a bath without starting to black out. I finished with the final accusation, '*You did it. You know you did. It's all true.*'

She left the house. Weeks later, I packed up and left town to start a new life, one that didn't include a mother.

Years later, I never found the right moment to tell her that upon learning she had tried to drown me and then stopped, or was stopped, marked the beginning of recovery for me. And then, it was too late to tell her I forgave her.

Every case is a reminder that dysfunctional family equals trouble. One kind or another. To this day, I prefer showers.

CHAPTER 8

SATURDAY, MAY 28TH

I stayed in bed listening to the steady drip of coffee until I was confident a full cup of coffee had brewed through. Determined to leave my shortcomings behind for the day, I took a moment to collect myself then lumbered out to the kitchen.

Filled to the brim, I peeked out the windows, cautiously, at the morning. A clear morning sky would warm to the high seventies, according to the morning weather report. I lifted my face to feel the sun. Very nice. I saturated myself in coffee as I leaned against the deck railing thinking about the relationships in this case so far. Carl's theory weighed heavy on my heart.

For Jake Mathews, the relationship with his dad changed when his mother died. Not necessarily in a destructive way, still questions about the family will be scrutinized including raised eyebrows about the kind of person he might have turned into due to his loss. Wrong conclusions will be drawn, blaming the victim. Did it have to go down like this? Not if I could do anything about it. Enter the fixer, alienated family member, re-born out of my own brokenness.

The ringing phone snapped me out of it. A wrong number, but it signaled it was time to move the day forward. I dressed quickly, grabbed my bag and keys, filled my travel mug with fresh coffee, and headed out.

As I pulled into the preserve parking lot, Deputy Bill walked toward me talking into his cell phone. My guess? He was letting Carl know I had arrived. He walked up to my van, rested his elbows through my open car window, and smiled brightly, something amusing he was pondering.

"Hi, Bill. You have some time for me today?"

"Yes, ma'am. I got orders to stick to you like glue on paper."

I smiled at the levity he must view his day's charge, my being underfoot as it were. I rolled up the windows and locked up my car.

"I'm to show you the access panel in the fence first. It's a bit of a walk." He eyed my shoes. "You okay to get a little dirt on those?"

I looked down at my feet. I should have made a better choice, like my KSwiss walkers, but hey, I'd opted for holiday spring wear instead, right down to open-toed sandals. Shoot. "No worries. I'm good," hoping to heck the thin straps wouldn't give way.

Trying to shake dirt and rocks out from between my toes as we walked resulted in Bill gaining a noticeable lead on me. He showed no sympathy. I could see a story being told later at my expense. I gave up and caught up to him. We stopped in front of an overgrown area with a grove of trees on the far side of the fence. I stepped closer as he pulled back at some of the brush.

He said, "I took pictures for evidence, if we need it. Don't worry about disturbing anything. We secured this fence panel so no one gets any ideas about driving in here anytime soon."

I pushed shrubbery aside exposing several broken branches and shoots sprouting from a snapped off section. I looked at Bill.

"Yep. Got a picture of that, too. Not recent cuts, though."

I nodded. The rough outline of a campfire was visible over the fence. "Find anything there?" I pointed to the campfire.

"A few recent tire tracks. If the killer used this spot last winter, any evidence is long gone. Still pretty muddy."

"Looks very secluded. You'd have to know it was here. Not something a tourist would stumble over."

"Campfire's not recent. Been cleaned out and the area picked up, nothing useful."

I nodded again. I looked back to the fence panel.

"So, this opening's big enough to drive a truck through then?"

He chuckled at my alibi humor. "Not a dually, but a decent sized pickup could do it. Wouldn't do the paint job any good, though."

I turned and started walking into the Mounds, telling Bill I'd meet him at his patrol car. He didn't look happy to have to report I took off on my own and started to protest.

Wanting to experience the Mounds in my own mind, but not at the expense of Bill's relationship with me or his boss, I said, "On second thought," spinning around to face him, "would you see if you can locate the phone number for the previous Ranger and catch up to me out here?"

Relieved, he said, "I'll catch up to you in a minute. I'll get it from the Ranger before he starts his tour. Please, stay out in the open, though." He jogged off in the direction of the Ranger's office.

I might have maybe five minutes alone. I hurried my pace. The crime scene tape was down. Only a hint of dark brown soil and shovel scrapes on the rocks marked where Jake's gravesite had been.

The sound of visitors beginning their trek through the trails filled the air. Walking, talking, and laughing, they made their way along the paved and rough trails lined with spring flowers and prairie grasses; picture perfect in the morning sun.

I took a deep breath and exhaled, trying to imagine what would move me to put a body out here. The Mounds had either a spiritual meaning or personal significance for the killer. This would remain my working theory. Place. Carl could work his holiday family drama theory.

Maybe we were making progress. With the discovery of the access panel, we had more information about opportunity to commit the crime. But, our evidence consisted of the dirt, now removed.

Skeletal remains, now taken. Ground ivy, source unknown. A weapon, perhaps known. I didn't have any idea about motive. And means? Everyone on the list had the means, with a little help.

I continued to take in the landscape, attempting to conjure up some abstract motive to fill the huge hole in my theory.

Minutes later, my solitude was interrupted by a group tour moving past me, led by Dan, one of many scheduled for the holiday weekend. Bill was at the back of the group. I heard a question about the body found here. Dan said something about it being a police matter and then, using animated gestures brought interest back to the history and mystery of the Mounds, effectively deflecting the other line of questioning. He was going to have his hands full this weekend.

One man in the tour slowed and looked past my feet to the area I was attempting to hide with my presence.

"Excuse me, ma'am," then shaking his head, "disturbing the peace," as he strolled by.

I hoped, for Dan's sake, the rest of the day's public sentiment would be as compassionate as this visitor's declaration.

Bill was at my elbow when I turned from watching Dan and his group move off through the fields. "Here's the number you wanted."

I put the piece of paper in my pocket. "Thanks, Bill. I'll call him later. Did you check for a gate key hanging in the office?"

"Yes, I checked this morning. Ranger says it's been hanging on the hook all along as far as he knew."

We spent a half hour more walking the fields as I worked to give life to my theory that this place was the key to solving the crime. I was out of empathic power. "So, off to the farm?"

Much to Bill's relief, we made our way to his patrol car. Carl must have warned him because he went straight to the front passenger door, holding it for me. I smiled, imagining what Bill must be thinking. All the personal quirks a career officer had to put up with the hired help.

Still contemplating the choice of place the killer made, I asked, "Remind me which counties border ours."

"That would be Lewis and Grays Harbor Counties, why?"

"Well, the Mounds extend to areas outside Thurston County. This outcropping is the tightest grouping on the aerial photos but in a secured protected field. Ya gotta wonder why here and not out in the less populated areas of the fields."

Thoughtful for a moment, his answer was practical. I'd learned to appreciate that about Carl and his team. "It may just be a random act in a place of convenience."

"Yeah. I suppose."

We approached the driveway of the house we didn't spend time at on my last trip down here with Carl. I was about to ask Bill about it when he said, "Carl wants us to talk to these folks. He said to tell you to "do your thing." You'd know what that meant."

"I do know. That's great. You and I are the interview team today then?"

"Yes, ma'am."

As we drove into the driveway, a number of cars lined the sides reminding me it was Memorial Day weekend. Barbecue gatherings were officially underway. No sooner were we out of the patrol car when, from around the corner of the house, a young man came toward us with a toddler in his arms.

"Can I help you?"

I stuck out my hand to be neighborly since what he was really saying was *'Can I help you leave'*. "Hi, I'm Lynzee Rose, and this is Deputy Bill…" I realized I didn't know Bill's last name and turned to see it on his uniform shirt, clear as day, "Symmons."

He didn't accept the greeting and instead hoisted his toddler over his shoulders using both hands to hold onto her legs. He widened his stance to say we weren't proceeding any further.

"We'll try to be quick if we can talk with you and your wife for a few minutes," I smiled again. "I didn't catch your name?"

"I didn't give it, as you very well know. What do you want here?"

Nice. This attitude had an all too familiar ring to it. "For starters, do you know Brooke Rivers?"

Bill's head jerked back. He had no idea where that had come from. I wasn't sure I did, but I pushed on. Bill looked back to our nameless tenant. I held my breath, hoping I'd hit a nerve questioning him about Brooke.

Without blinking, he asked, "What, exactly, do you want here?"

Bill didn't like the aggressive stance our citizen had taken, and the tone this young man was taking with us had hit his last good nerve. He said, "We're investigating a murder at Mima Mounds, as you may have heard, and as part of that investigation, we're here talking to all the Mounds Preserve neighbors. How about you help us by answering our questions." He put his hands on his hips, right index finger coming to rest on the snap of his holster and handcuffs, ready to take it to the next level if he didn't receive the cooperation his body language was now demanding. His actions did not go without notice. Point made.

"My name is Brian Cooper and my wife's name is Amber. We live here and have done nothing to warrant a visit by the County Sheriff's department and whoever *you* are."

I think he knew more about me than he was letting on. "Do you know Brooke, or don't you?" Without Carl here, I found myself both good cop and bad cop, not the intermediary I wanted to be.

From the back of the house, walking in her annoyed manner, came Brooke. She did not look happy to see me, of that I was sure.

"Brooke," I waved and smiled in her direction, "You mentioned you camped down this way. Took a chance you weren't the only one who liked Scatter Creek, seeing it's so close by. So, you're friends with the Coopers here?"

"That's correct. Why are you here? Are you following me?"

"Following you? Goodness, no. Still investigating the murder of your recent boyfriend, yes. I hope you're happy about that."

"Of course. These are my friends. They all knew Jake and mourn his loss, as do I," she added.

"Why don't we all sit down and talk about how you're all connected."

Hearing no objection, I started for the back yard. Bill followed Brooke and Brian.

After a long half hour, we had names and relationships of the ten people gathered at the Cooper homestead. Bill took a bunch of notes. We learned they were all in the same coven. Brian and Amber rented the place, having seen it available on the way back from one of their outings. We talked about connections with Jake and got an understanding about the whereabouts of everyone the day the bones were removed from the Morgue. No one had anything negative to say about Jake.

Neither Bill or I asked them if they knew anything about the small campfire area we'd just left. I could hear Carl's voice from here, warning us off that subject with this bunch.

Bill checked in with Carl who told him we would do more research on the group if it became necessary. Bill and I stood up ready to take our leave when I noticed a building out back. I pointed to the barn. "I'd like to take a look around." I'm not sure I had authority to march into the barn, with or without Bill.

Seeing us walking toward the barn, Brian ran up to us. "Don't you guys need a warrant to snoop around here?"

"I'll rustle one up." Bill stopped walking and waited.

Brian stepped to the side and waved us forward. "If you tell me what you're looking for, maybe we can save some time here. Then I can get back to my guests."

Opening the doors, an exquisitely maintained cabinet shop came into view. Nothing was laying out in plain view. We would need that warrant.

Bill and I made eye contact. No way would we be able to look for a murder weapon without spilling the beans. Brian told us he was a carpenter cabinetmaker. He'd have many tools. Perhaps even a scratch awl.

Bill walked off and made the call.

I took the next leap. "Where do you keep your truck?"

"What's my truck have to do with anything?"

Bingo.

"We'll decide what we need to see and what we don't. Your truck?" Bill had returned. He was becoming very effective obtaining useful information out of Brian.

"It's behind the barn."

Curious about this, I asked, "Any particular reason you keep it out of view?"

"Amber says it's an eyesore. So, I drive it around when I need to load up for a delivery. There a crime in that?"

Neither of us answered.

Bill caught my eye and lifted his chin pointing in the direction of his patrol car. I nodded.

Returning with a camera, he took down the license number and snapped pictures of the truck from all sides. A faded yellow mustard color; it was well-used and no stranger to hard work. He did a slow walk around, looking for newer scratch marks he could differentiate from the well-aged ones on this old GMC. He checked the bed of the truck and took more pictures then jogged back to his car to run the plates.

I decided to try one more time to develop some kind of positive relationship with Brian. "You say Jake was a friend to your group. Why is it no one here cares enough to help us find out what happened to him?"

He dropped the bravado, offering his take on the matter. "Look. We all liked Jake well enough. We were surprised when he didn't show up over Yule. We were glad Brooke was dating, moving on from Mark's death. None of us had any reason to do him harm. It's not who we are or what we are about."

"Mark Rivers?"

"Rivers is Brooke's name. Mark's last name was Burrows."

Was Mark a member of the coven?"

"Yes. He was. We all miss him." Looking down at his boots,

he moved the rock around under the sole of one of them before speaking. "I'll see if I can convince the coven to put some energy on this. I'll ask to hold a circle. See if we can come up with answers for you. That's the best I can do."

"Good enough." This time he shook my extended hand. Bill returned and gave him a card with the office phone number.

On our walk back to the patrol car, Bill let his relief show. "I'm glad you didn't mention the awl tool specifically. Thanks for reading my mind. I should have said."

"I'm pretty good at mind reading."

"Called for a team to come down with a search warrant. Mr. Cooper's day is not going to get any better anytime soon. We could have had him show us around, but Carl wanted things handled officially. Their hostility is their own undoing. They should be here within the hour to go through the garage. They'll look for anything resembling the murder weapon. Hanging around any longer would only put them on alert. We'll just have to take our chances."

We loaded up and drove to the Connor farm. I was dreading this visit. I like Ralph. I still felt the sting of what happened to Joe. I did not want to see another hospital visit in anyone's future, but especially not Ralph's. I vowed to tread carefully.

Bill turned his head to me as we drove and asked, "How'd you know that bunch were part of Brooke's witch group?"

"I didn't. The predisposed hostility was familiar. I took a chance. It paid off."

"I ran the plates on the truck. It's clean and as far as I can tell, so's Brian."

We pulled up to Ralph's house and went over the rules we would follow. No specific mention of either the awl, dirt, or the access panel. We still had to talk to Scott. Carl didn't want Ralph giving him a heads up. Bill asked me what I thought so far.

"You mean that group back there?" pointing toward the farm we just left.

He nodded.

"I don't see a motive for anyone in the group. Maybe Brooke operating on her own. Would they help her? Maybe they would. I don't expect we'll hear from Brian about any future help. Worst-case scenario is some ritual went wrong, an accident and cover up occurred. But not murder."

"We for sure won't get any voluntary help from any of them from here on out once the warrant is served and the barn is searched."

"There was one good outcome out of it for me. The whole group says Jake wasn't with them during Yule, including Christmas Eve. We questioned them separately. True, they could all be covering for each other. It didn't feel that way, though."

"Don't agree with you. I think they're behavior is very suspicious. All of them."

"I'll put my reputation, what little I have in this area, on this killing having a spiritual element." The second part to my theory was officially out in the open.

"Spiritual as in Native American spiritual?"

"I'm not going to open that door. That'll bring the Commissioner down on us like flies to horse poo."

I saw he appreciated my 'stick to' reference from his earlier reference.

We walked up the porch stairs and knocked on the door. Ralph opened it a few long minutes later and invited us into the living room. A blanket was draped across the chair where he'd evidently been napping. Looking around apologetically, he showed us to the sofa across from where he sat himself down.

"Did we wake you? If so, we can come back, Ralph. We were in the neighborhood and thought we'd stop in and see how you were doing."

He looked tired. I couldn't help thinking something recently occurred bringing on a sleepless night.

"You okay?"

"A little down. Disappointed. Thought my son was going to come spend some time with me over the holiday weekend. Said he was tied up out of town."

"You know, since our last visit, we learned that your son is Scott. He's a supervisor for construction projects for a hotel chain, right?"

Bill's face showed concern as to how this was going to play out. He gave me a look of caution. I wasn't supposed to mention Scott. I gave him a quick wink meant to let him know I knew what I was doing.

"You know my son?" Ralph lit up at the mention.

"Haven't had the pleasure of meeting him. He's helping us with our investigation by phone. Seems our victim worked for him."

"Now, I didn't know that. Scott doesn't talk to me about his work with the hotel company."

"Why's that, I wonder."

"I was upset when he left his architect job in Seattle. Still don't know why he chose hard labor over a soft chair and desk job after all the farm work he did here as a boy."

"That would mean a whole new tool set from drafting tools, wouldn't it?"

Out of the corner of my eye, Bill was moving nervously forward on the sofa.

"Yeah. He put away his drafting pencil for a carpenter pencil. And, he went and traded his Saab for a truck, too. I offered him all my old tools, but he wanted brand new ones. Told him old ones are better, stronger materials used in the old days. But, nope. Didn't want 'em."

"I agree with you about the old days, Ralph. I have my dad's old tools. I've been restoring them to their original condition; they were left in a damp environment for many years. Dad used to be a carpenter before he turned commercial fisherman."

"You don't say. Would you like to see what I have? I put 'em to good use over the years. Built this house with those tools. Don't have much use for them anymore, but they're still in real good condition.

I get a kick out of keeping them around for the memories. In a way, I'm glad he didn't take them."

"Maybe he knew that all along."

Ralph perked up at this reasoning.

"I'd love to see those tools. How about you, Bill? We have a little time, don't we?"

Bill stood up saying, "If you're sure you want to, sir. We don't want to impose."

"No imposing. It's an invitation. I'd be honored if you accept."

We were covered, but caution was the word of the day. "We were just talking with your neighbors, the Cooper family. Brian is a cabinetmaker. You have a chance to meet them?"

"Can't say as I've had the pleasure. Might just stop by one of these first days."

The three of us strolled out to the barn where we discovered a multitude of tools for carpentry. Saws, squares, hammers, wrenches and snips all set out carefully on specially constructed shelving. And, all out in plain view. Carl will be pleased. I was careful not to touch anything.

"You've got a nice collection here, Ralph."

We walked around with Ralph as he picked up, talked about, and then set down various tools, all with a story. Bill and I stayed behind him. We weren't going to start rifling through things until Carl and Scott had talked. We'd then be doing a search or ruling this family out.

Ralph rested his hands on his workbench and said, "Well, I had more. Guess he decided he did want some of them after all."

That raised both Bill's and my eyebrows. I said, "Do you know what's missing?" I knew I was treading on dangerous ground.

"Not for sure. Just odds and ends, I think. I'll call him. See if he took them."

Not good. I screwed up. Quickly recovering, I said, "Perhaps wait til he comes over. Be easier to do a walk through with him, especially since you're not certain what's missing. If it wasn't Scott, you may have had an intruder. Both you should take action then and report it." I hated doing this to him, but I had a misstep, and the ball was in my court to correct it. I couldn't have him talking to Scott about missing tools. Carl wouldn't let me out again without him.

Bill looked like he was holding his breath. Finally, Ralph spoke.

"S'pose you're right. He said he'd be back up this way Tuesday, I'll wait to talk him then." He looked up quickly and asked, "Say, how you folks doing with that murder investigation? The boys down at the corner market are all wondering."

Bill breathed a sigh of relief. "Not making much progress, Mr. Connors. Might just have to throw it in with all those other mysteries of the Mounds."

"Yeah, well, there's a lot of those around," he chuckled to himself.

I touched on one final piece, determined not to blow it. "Did you live here when the fence went up around the Mounds?"

"Oh sure. It was a big deal getting that special designation. Thought it would put Littlerock on the map. But being out in the middle of nowhere didn't make us somewhere just 'cause of a tourist designation. I suppose if we had put up some of those signs across the State like they did with that Wall Drug dud we might have seen more action."

I knew what he saying. Drive across the Badlands and the promise of something great coming is slapped up on billboards for a hundred miles across the dismal, barren terrain. And then to find a tourist trap you wished you'd missed.

Ralph left the barn with us in tow, stopping to face the outstretched prairies, full of mounds. "A bunch of the locals went over for a gander when it was dedicated. Looks the same way it always has, only more official. Several farmers then wished they could have made a nice chunk of change selling land off to the government."

"Lots of good history here. You have a nice location, Ralph."

Bill was anxious for us to be moving along. "Gotta get going, Ralph. You take care of yourself, now."

We walked to the car. "Thanks for the save, Bill. I nearly screwed up badly."

"You got out of it all on your own without any help from me."

He dropped me back at my car while he went to see how the search was going at the Cooper barn. I set off to sort plant out the rest of my day. I wasn't out of the entrance road before my phone rang. I pulled over.

"Can you meet me for lunch on your way home?"

It was Carl. Big surprise. "Sure. Let's go to South Bay Grill. You know the place?"

"Yep, on South Bay Road. See you in a few."

The drive was easy. Most people already at the places they wanted to be for the weekend. I took back roads to avoid any residual freeway traffic. He was waiting when I pulled in.

Taking advantage of a sunny day, we sat outside and ordered the specialty, pulled pork nachos. He had a casual look to him and noticed me noticing. "My folks are here for the holiday weekend."

That explained him being tied up.

We both ordered a beer, Blue Moon, a nice white Belgian complete with fresh orange slices.

"How nice. Surprise visit? What are you doing here with me?"

"Truth be told, I needed a break. Thought lunch with you would be just the ticket."

My questioning expectant look brought no further clarification.

"Thought we could coordinate our schedules for next week. Folks are leaving first thing Monday morning. You okay to come into the office, say, around eleven?"

Working on an official holiday. I guess I could. I had no plans. "Sure," thinking we could have done this part over the phone. "Are they okay? Your folks, I mean?"

Seeing I wasn't going to drop it, he took a deep breath and let it out, "I don't know why they decided to visit. It's been quite a while since they've been up this way, or even left California. I don't make a good tour guide."

"Perhaps getting older and wanting to feel like they are still able to come and go on their own has something to do with it."

"I hadn't thought of that."

"One day, you'll be making decisions for them. Enjoy them and their independence while you can, Carl."

We toasted life and dug in.

CHAPTER 9

SUNDAY, MAY 29TH

"Hello, Ranger Baker? It's Lynzee Rose with the Sheriff's Department. Do you remember me from yesterday?" I'd waited til noon to call in case he attended church in the morning. Didn't want him to think I was a heathen on top of what some of my next questions might lead him to think.

"Sure. Sure. I remember. You like those stories about the Mounds," he chuckled.

Not being what I hoped had stuck with him, I went ahead and confessed. "I did like your stories, yes. That would be me."

"What can I do to for you this fine Sunday morning?"

"As you know, we're working through what happened in the Mounds. We don't have any good leads yet, the reason it happened and all." Shoot. I forgot how much we'd said about the evidence in the case. I was stumbling so I pulled back and changed the subject. "One thing you said the other day got me thinking. We're looking at all the theories floating around about the Mounds, whatever their source."

"Oh, well then, how can I help?"

"You said something about the *tear shape* of mounds, remember?"

139

"And, you're wondering what I meant."

"Yes. Is it tied to a Native American spiritual legend or what?"

He chuckled again. "Wish I could say it had that kind of importance. Fact is, it's more local than that."

"How so?"

"Don't know if I mentioned it earlier, but I grew up in Littlerock. We kids came up with all kinds of ideas about what those fields were all about. Don't know if you knew this or not, but Littlerock is part of the Thurston County Bible Belt."

"No, I didn't know there was such a thing here."

"Informal designation. For years local congregations referred to the Mounds as *'God's tears'*. Tears He shed with the sacrifice of his Son for us all. We even set out to find maps and count them; see if we could apply it to some of the number groups you find in the Bible."

I didn't want to get into Biblical theories. "Is that still a current theory, the tears I mean, for the locals?"

"Not so much. We didn't have video games or the internet to amuse us; we used our imaginations instead. Put them to good use." He chuckled to himself again.

"So you didn't end up with a count of them, then. I can see where counting mounds would have been a pretty big task for a group of kids."

"When you factor in how many we have just in the County alone, and then add those in multiple states, it turned out to be impossible. But, as kids, it took a while to figure out Littlerock's mounds weren't the center of the universe, if you know what I mean."

"I do. Thanks. One more thing. You said you grew up in Littlerock. Do you know Ralph Connors?"

"Oh, sure. He's been around forever. Lost his wife Christmas Eve maybe five years ago. A real blow for him. Things were never the same for that family when she passed. Been ages since I last spoke to him."

Really, I thought. Another family holiday loss for Carl's theory.

How many more will turn up as we work this case. I'd better leave that one alone for now. "Did the local folks ever spend much time helping out at the Mounds once it was made an official park?"

"At first, then not so much. Most of the folks here have mounds in their own back yards and kick themselves for not trying to cash in on the deal themselves. A few of them helped, from time to time, readying the place for tourists. Then, they drifted off to manage their own lives once the newness of the place wore off."

I checked the time and decided to end the call. "Gare, you've been a great help. Can I call you again if I have any more questions?"

"Of course. It's been a pleasure. Glad I could help."

"Bye now."

I barely had my finger off the call end button when I hit speed dial. Carl didn't answer so I left a quick message to call me when he could. I remembered, too late, he was in the middle of a family visit and regretted leaving the message. It could have waited til Monday morning.

I turned my attention to getting my house, yard, and refreshments ready for this afternoon's event. I set up things the way Lori had instructed then cut up fruit and put it on a platter. While defrosting the pink lemonade, I located several pitchers for the concoction. Mixing it all together, I added a smidge of Rose's Limejuice, to sweeten it up a bit and then tasted it. Yum.

It was one o'clock. Lori would be along in about thirty minutes, her time clock based on when she left her home, not when she was due. It took a couple of meetings to figure it out; so, I planned accordingly. Sure enough, she pulled in when expected. We set up snacks, drinks, ice, paper plates, and plastic cups. I sampled her banana bread. It was as I expected, fabulous. Just as we finished, the Poker Run official's cart rolled up.

When the dust settled, and the last cart took off for the next stop along their seven-stop game route, it was time to sit back and take part in the leftovers. I went for the punch. She went to her car and pulled out a hidden stash of goodies. Listening to the carts slamming to another stop along the line, we dug in. With the help of some of the good punch, I forgot all about the crime. We laughed til the sun went down as she told of things to come in this annual event. She said after the poker wheel spun for the seventh time, the players head off to the Clubhouse Bar and start the serious task of more drinking and reducing hands down to the best five card poker hand. Celebration stories will be told of the card almost dealt, the near miss on the road, and the food and drink shared along the way. All, til the stories bore little resemblance to the facts, reduced to folklore of Poker Runs past.

CHAPTER 10

MONDAY, MAY 30TH

Rolling out of bed, eyes gluey from sleep, I found my way to a hot shower, then called Carl. He answered on the first ring.

"You okay? I didn't hear back from you last night. Did you get my message? I was ready to call out the troops."

Since I was still a little hung over from too much punch, I was really glad he hadn't driven out to see for himself. "Oh, you were not. I'm sorry I bothered you yesterday. It was late when I got your message, then...," Changing the subject, I asked, "Did you have a nice visit with your folks?"

"Yeah, it turned out fine. Thank you for your insight. I took a drive up to Mt. Rainer. They'd never been there. They liked it a lot. Phone was out of range when you called. Many dead zones up that way. Everything all right?"

"Everything's fine. I had some thoughts I wanted to share with you. They can wait til I see you. No problems here yesterday either, so that's a plus. Be there at eleven, okay?"

"Yep. See you soon."

*   *   *

I stepped off the elevator and located Bill returning to his desk. Good. He was off Mounds duty today. I handed him one of three coffees I'd stopped for on my way. This one to thank him for babysitting me yesterday. He looked tired. I felt sure all of us on this case had the same look. Taking in striking features I hadn't noticed yesterday, his dark complexion and jet black hair set off a strong square jaw and large cheekbones. Definitely in the handsome category.

"Thanks, Ms. Rose. Much appreciated this morning." Tipping his cup in my direction, he said, "Good coffee is like a good woman." He smiled up at me then started to apologize.

I raised a hand to stop him. "Okay. I'll bite. Why is good coffee like a good woman?"

"I think I shouldn't say, sorry." His face reflecting dread of a sensitivity refresher course in the near future. He squared his shoulders then put the cup to his lips, nodding as the hot liquid met with approval.

"Well, enjoy both, then." I gave him a high five and moved on to Carl's office.

Carl had watched the interchange, but his eye were set on what was in my hand. I promptly deposited one in front of him, much to his relief. That left me the one I'd been working on. "What cha got?" I pointed to the fresh stack on his desk.

"Tom met with a couple members of the crew; I'm reading his report now. They weren't thrilled coming in on a holiday weekend. Perhaps they came just out of curiosity, something to share around a barbecue later." The two regulars didn't know Jake very well. One from Labor Ready didn't even recognize his picture."

"Did they know anything about the dirt?"

"All said the unused dirt goes to anyone presenting an official letter."

"What does the letter say?"

"None of them read passed the first few lines. They looked for the Inn logo and a subject line that said topsoil removal. Then they let them in. All offered alibis for December twenty-fourth, which will be easy enough to check out if we need to. They were with family." His look said, 'chalk that up for my side' to our recent debate about where people spend their holidays.

"Any progress with where Scott was for that day?" I chose not to challenge the count.

"Apparently, Scott's not on a time clock. Doesn't punch in like the hourly guys."

"Do you think we'll see Scott tomorrow?"

"Mr. Monroe is still talking to his corporate lawyers. If Scott shows up, we're good."

"Hmmm. I thought we had a letter giving us permission to talk with Scott. Why the resistance?"

"The letter gave permission for Scott to talk to us about past employees related to a construction job last winter. I think the hotel is concerned about their corporation liability. Scott's management, as you pointed out, and a current employee. They may want a lawyer with him before he talks to us."

"Well, on another note, I have some news about the Connors' family you'll want to hear."

"I'll bite. What?" He looked up over his coffee pressing it against his lips, a bit of a smile letting me know he heard my exchange with Bill.

"Do *you* know how good coffee is like a good woman?"

"Maybe later, although, I'm certain you could come up with something on your own if you thought about it."

I wasn't going to now, but I accepted that challenge. "What we know is that December twenty-fourth is the last time we know that anyone talked with Jake. It's a reoccurring theme." From Carl's look, I had some convincing work to do.

"Theme? This is a murder investigation. We don't do *'themes'*. You talking about facts or feelings now?" His voice testy with fatigue.

"Both." Okay, that didn't help. I explained, "I called Gare Baker, the former Ranger, he knows Ralph Connors, by the way." I summed up Gare's story about the early years of the Mounds and the local kids.

"Nice local lore, but what does that have to do with December twenty-fourth or solving this case for that matter?"

"Well, in passing, Gare told me the Connors family hadn't been the same since Ralph's wife died five years ago on December twenty-fourth."

"And we would tie that in how?"

"I think we should look at when Jake's mom died."

Carl sank back in his chair and waited for me to fold.

I didn't and crossed my arms in front of me to let him know I wasn't moving on the subject.

"That idea is pretty far out there, even for you."

Deciding not to be offended by that, I explained, "Yesterday at the Mounds got me thinking outside the box, the perspective I was talking about with the trees, remember?" I didn't wait for an answer. "I came up with my own theory on the motive for this murder."

"Really? And that is?"

"It's the Mounds itself. The place. There's either a spiritual or a personal attachment for the killer."

He opened a file. Then, looking up he said, "The press conference was just days ago. Someone could still come forward who talked or met with Jake after Christmas." He poked at the keyboard bringing his computer to life. A few minutes passed. He looked up, making direct eye contact. "Her name is Gretchen Mathews. She died on December twenty-fourth."

I nearly jumped with renewed confidence.

Carl pondered that information, then said, "That may move Scott up on the suspect list, or it might actually put him on a possible target list, which I'm hoping we don't start mapping out next."

"If nothing else, it's the reason Scott and Jake connected with each other. It may be the common denominator, the issue. Scott may be a link he isn't aware of himself. We really have to talk to him."

"We don't have enough to bring him in as a suspect. And, we don't have enough to put him under protection, either. But, the information gives us another direction to explore, like we need another one of those." He scratched his chin. "Deaths around the Christmas holidays aren't all that infrequent, sad to say. We've been down this road. You know my theory on this murder. Family or friends." He thought some more, then asked, "How do the deaths of two moms years ago and years apart tie in?"

I was sure he wasn't going to like where I was going, but I took this as my opening. "It was something Gare Baker said about how many mound fields we have throughout the country." I pulled a map out of my bag. With some effort concentrating after Lori left, I found it online. My printer didn't do the best job, but it was easy enough to see the substantial mound fields located throughout the States. "Look at this map with me." I handed it to him.

He took hold of the map, studied it, and then set it down. "So, what do we do with this?"

"I'm starting to think this crime is bigger than Thurston County. We should check missing persons in states with mound fields. Single young men missing on or about December twenty-fourth who were living in areas near mound prairie fields when they were last seen."

Carl came out from behind his desk with my map in hand. We both sat down at the conference table. He said, "Good Lord, Lynzee. How far back would you want to look? Even a few years back could produce hundreds of results." He exhaled loudly. "You want me to contact the alien abduction bunch and get their input, too?"

He wasn't onboard. "I'm not talking about alien abductions." At least I didn't think I was. "I'm suggesting a computer search in a few of these states here," I said pointing to the map. "Single, Caucasian men in their early thirties, say back three to five years. We can change the parameters if there are no hits."

"Change parameters to what or where? The entire country?

The entire male population? You know how many man hours are involved here?"

I pointed to my map again. "Please. How 'bout we start with Colorado and Wyoming. Less population in those states and, hopefully, fewer missing men."

Carl leaned forward, concentrating on how many counties were involved. He straightened himself and leaned back in his chair. His look told me he was contemplating whether this exercise would result in a call out before his boss. He pointed to Oklahoma then went to his desk. He thumbed through a huge directory.

"I know this is a lot to ask, Carl. I'll understand if you decide it's we don't have the resources, but don't say it's not viable. We're out of practical angles."

Not looking up and talking mostly to himself he said, "If I agree to look into this angle, we see what turns up from missing persons reports using basic online resources only." He stepped over to his window observing his team working at their desks then turned back to me offering, "I'll give three detectives each a state of focus." He went to the door, stopping before he opened it. Burdened with a look of dread, he added, "You know what you're suggesting?"

He didn't want to use the 'S' word. He didn't have to. "Carl, I haven't learned anything that tells me Jake died due to a family fall out. Honestly, if it was some freak pagan accident, you don't bury someone in a field of little hills, you go for help. Equally, nothing's jumping out as motive for a personal vendetta." I stopped talking and looked over at the white board. "But, I agree. We should continue to look at the people on the list, but expand it to include the guys in Jake's unit." Breathing deeply, I let go of the rest of my theory and emphasized my final point. "I don't think we're going to find only one body turning up buried in a mound field."

"I think what we're going to find, if you're right, is a jurisdictional mine field on our hands." Carl went out to talk to Bill, taking my map along. They went over to the copier machine, talking along the way.

Shortly, he reappeared next to me. "Okay. Bill's going to spearhead a team and pull any missing person reports, on or around Christmas in Colorado, Wyoming, and Oklahoma."

Now it was my turn to exhale. I did. I rubbed my eyes, suddenly feeling tired.

Carl sat on the edge of his desk. "I don't see one incident as setting a pattern. Why focus on our victim profile? It's just one case."

"Honestly, it's because both Jake and Scott are near the same age, have a similar look, lost their mothers on the same day, and one of them is dead. It's not much, I know."

Resignedly, he said, "We'll run printouts on anyone we find fitting Jake's general description." He sighed, "I pray to God you're wrong on this, Lynzee."

"Me, too."

"I appreciate your looking at this scenario, Carl. I know it's a bit out there."

He grabbed his jacket and keys. "How about we tackle that other angle you mentioned?"

"The Army?"

Carl walked across the room and picked up the phone. By the time he hung up, we were out the door to Ft. Lewis-McChord base to meet with the day-to-day operations manager of war-fighting units, Colonel Cameron Cooper. "Jake's squad sergeant redeployed to Iraq. The Colonel is the one Joe talked to; so, that's who we're going to see."

"Does everybody around here work the holidays?" I asked nobody in particular as we loaded into Carl's official rig.

"So it would seem," Carl commiserated. "Colonel said this is a big day on the base."

"Oh yeah. I guess it would be."

"I just caught him at his desk. He'll give us a few minutes. Then he's got places to be."

The drive North to the base took twenty minutes. Getting onto the base and into the Colonel's office took another half hour.

When we were finally seated in the Colonel's office, coffee in hand, he launched into the rules on what he would and would not discuss. It wasn't just the coffee that had gone cold by the time he finished. I was beginning to think this was a wasted trip.

Carl cut through the red tape with, "I can understand your position, Colonel. You have to understand mine. I have one of your own, dead. Killed. Pieces of this investigation have lead us right here."

"How so?" The Colonel was suddenly interested.

"Jake and Paul were in non combatant posts together, working in operations, transportation, I think it was. We have Jake dating the widow of Mark Burrows, Brooke. Mark happened to be a combat field medic and known to both Jake and Paul."

"Okay."

"I understand Mark took his own life. I'd like to know the circumstances and how Mark, Paul, and Jake were connected in Iraq and here on post."

"I'm going to spare you the top secret rigmarole of our work in Iraq and say this, when I took the call from Joe Mathews, I was very interested. We took a serious look into the matter."

Carl pushed on. "I'm aware Joe filed a missing person's report with you."

"Of sorts, yes. I told him that his son was a civilian. I had no authority to pursue it. I agreed to look into it, informally, in part because Jake and Mark were in the same unit, but mostly because I needed to know if I had another suicide on my hands. When I learned, from your press conference, that Jake's death was a murder, not a suicide; I breathed a sigh of relief. Although, I realize saying that out loud sounds calloused." He paused, thinking to himself. He went to his desk and opened a file that had been there since we walked in. He pulled out a two-page form document and brought it over. Handing it to Carl, he said, "I made you a copy of what we were able to learn about Jake's post service activities. I'm afraid it's not much."

I scooted my chair closer so I could look at the document as Carl flipped through. Both of us looked up as the Colonel spoke.

"Let me say this about Mark Burrows in relationship to your case. His work in Iraq was unlike the work Jake and Paul were doing. There would have been little opportunity for them to get to know each other. Different interests once they all came back, too. Mark re-enlisted while Paul and Jake did not. And, as far as my investigation went into this matter, there's no one in Mark's unit that had a grudge around Jake's interest in Brooke. Which brings us to Mark's death." He took a deep breath, and then continued. "We look hard at service related suicides. Our own base statistics are high enough that I scrutinize every non-combatant death personally. In Mark's case, he suffered from PTSD. He was having difficulty coping with the day-to-day aspect of war and his role. We thought his treatment was successful. We were, obviously, very wrong."

Carl asked, "And in Jake's case?"

"I would have been extremely surprised to find that Jake had taken his own life. He'd discharged from the service and started a new career. His friend, Paul, discharged and enrolled in school. They both moved on."

I raised my hand to interrupt. "Sir, about Mark's wife, Brooke. We met with her; and, frankly, her attitude around her husband's death, and her boyfriend's death, lack emotional attachment. Can you shed some light on that?" It was another piece of this case I couldn't reconcile.

"I'm sure you heard that Brooke got a ton of grief regarding the lack of decorum she showed at her husband's funeral. His death had nothing to do with his marriage to Brooke and nothing to do with Jake's time in the service or his friendship with Brooke." He paused, and then asked, "I'm not sure I should comment any further about Brooke."

I wanted more. " Colonel, we know a lot about her already. We know her father was in the service. She spent time in England. She changed her name from Anderson to Rivers for some reason. She didn't use her husband's name. She is a Wiccan. She dated Jake. She didn't like Paul. She's a nurse." I left out those things about her personality that were my own take on her.

He hesitated. "You know quite a bit."

Carl was sensing the red tape going up again. "Colonel, this is a murder investigation of a soldier on U.S. turf. Any pertinent information you have that would shed some light on it, you need to share with us."

The Colonel bit his lip, not saying what he was thinking about who was on who's turf. He went over to the window behind his desk. As he looked out, he put his hands on his hips. Not the kind of body language conducive to sharing.

The door was closing; I came at him from a different direction. "Colonel, are you a father?"

He turned away from the window and studied me. He gave a quick shake of his head and sat down at his desk. Looking back and forth between Carl and me, he made a decision. "Okay. This is off record. I'll deny it was ever said. Are we clear?"

"Clear," Carl and I said together. I wanted to add *'crystal'* but this was not a good time for movie trivia.

"Brooke utilizes our base counseling services on Tuesdays. Has for over a year."

Second or third time in this case I nearly fell off my chair. Scratch her off the suspect list for body snatching. I'm guessing he knew more about the counseling story, but the look on the Colonel's face warned me away from asking. Curious Brooke said she was running errands rather than tell us she was at an appointment. A light bulb went on.

"Colonel, is Brooke an only child?"

There was a long pause before he responded. "She had a brother. Killed in Kosovo a few years back in a freak accident. It left scars on the family. I believe that is when you'll find her rebirth under a different last name and a new choice in faith practices."

Carl asked, "This counseling you mentioned. What is the current status of Brooke's emotional or mental well being?" Not satisfied with the limits of his first question, he added, "Do you think Brooke could be connected to Jake's death?"

A loaded question. We sat in silence while the Colonel formed his response. It was brief. "I hope not."

Carl opened his mouth to protest.

The Colonel opened his own mouth in objection saying, "I know you're trying to find out who killed Jake. Here's my assessment. No one in Mark's unit should be on your suspect list. We found no evidence of animosity toward Jake over his involvement with Brooke. He was a fellow soldier first. That value matters most to men who serve their country. However, I am willing to make arrangements for you to speak with members of Mark's unit, those still on base, if you'd like."

"Generous of you. I think that would be helpful. But, back to Brooke?" Carl leaned forward leading the Colonel back to his question.

"What concerns me about Brooke is that she has lived through so much loss in her young life. A brother she was close to. Her husband. And now her boyfriend. I know the family, as you may have guessed, so I can speak with some authority on this subject, off record of course."

Carl and I nodded in support of the Colonel continuing.

"When Mark took his life, Brooke was devastated. She did not see it coming. None of us did. When Brooke entered another relationship so soon after her husband's death, a flag went up, a signal to her family she needed to enter counseling. They convinced her."

"Is it feasible Brooke snapped when she thought she was losing Jake?" I already knew what he was going to say.

"I hope not."

"You said Brooke's brother was in Kosovo. He was in the service then?"

"Yes, he was."

Did Brooke's brother hold a similar position in the Army as her husband?" Still hoping to start connecting some dots.

"No. Brooke's brother was Battalion Chaplain." With that, the Colonel said that was all the time he had for us.

Carl turned back as we were leaving. "Colonel, I understand the unit came together to cover the cost of a memorial service today here on base. I want you to know, we will make this right."

With a half smile of appreciation, he dismissed us. "Thank you, Detective. Now, I need to go talk with them and tell them we'll be rescheduling that service."

We were quiet, thoughtful, on our return drive, a lot to consider.

Traffic was heavy with first of the season campers returning home, it was after two when we stepped into the County elevator.

"Carl, you think Brooke changed her name and became a Wiccan because of her Christian brother's death in Kosovo?"

"I think I'm going to see if Pastor Mike can come in and chat with us today."

Half an hour later, we had Club sandwiches for three and all the goodies.

Pastor Mike knew his way around the department, greeted by several of Carl's team on his way through. He dove, unceremoniously, into the sandwich. Between mouthfuls, he kept his eyes on us. Breaking our silence while opening a bag of chips, he said, "Thanks for lunch, Carl. You both look like something is troubling you. How can I help?"

I didn't know about Carl, but I needed no further encouragement. Hoping not to be struck by lightning, I eased in slowly. "We learned Brooke had a brother who was a Chaplain oversees and died suddenly. That's when she changed her name and joined the Wiccan faith."

"Is there a question in there?"

More confident in his standing with questioning a pastor about a murder investigation, Carl took over. "People break from their faith for a lot of excuses, some of them even reasons. Her break from a Christian family, name change included, has us both wondering about her emotional and mental state. I think we're trying to understand if she is capable of a more serious break. One that includes murder."

Carl filled Mike in on our visit north.

Cautiously, Mike responded, "Loss is managed in many ways. Her struggles with her Christian background and the timing of her brother's death may have been a factor in her leaving the faith, but I doubt it was the only one. God gets blamed for much *not* of his own making." He scanned our faces seeing expectant looks, and then answered with, "I think the question is: Was losing her brother and husband a trigger for murder if she believed Jake was abandoning her? My answer: It's possible." Pastor Mike ended with, "I would very much like to talk with Brooke when this is behind us."

My disappointment showed. I counted on the Pastor for a miracle, or at least, some divine inspiration.

Pastor Mike watched us struggling. "That Brooke seeks a spiritual connection with a higher being is a good thing. We haven't lost her. She'll be back, sooner than we think. Her Wicca belief system isn't going to give her what she needs most, connection with the great Healer and a loving relationship with her true Maker. That's the only way to fill the dark hole we all carry around inside us."

Carl showed relief.

I was hoping to solve a murder, not save a soul.

The phone rang. Carl took the call leaving me to fill the conversational gap. "Carl mentioned this thing about your church and its relationship to '*social justice*' rather than '*social action*'. What's the difference and why the distinction, one over the other?"

"Social justice relates to quality of life, one of the goals we have for mankind. Social action, on the other hand, is what it takes to get that justice. Unfortunately, it often gets a bad rap from activists pushing personal or political agendas, which are not necessarily for the common good. Clear as mud?"

"Actually, yes. I think. Which were you a part of in Israel?"

Pastor Mike let out a laugh catching the attention of anyone within hearing range. "Touché, Ms. Rose. Touché. *That* was out and out protesting. That's what that was." He continued chuckling to himself.

Carl came back to the table. "More bad news. The dirt from the Littlerock store did not match the sample from the crime scene."

"Or good news." My infrequent Pollyanna side showing. "Elimination is good. That still leaves us with construction site dirt."

"Bill picked up a sample from the hotel grounds on his return trip from the Mounds Saturday. I put a rush on it."

"You got anything more for me?" Pastor Mike began clearing off the table.

"Yes, actually I have one more thing. What do ground ivy and beer have in common?" I didn't know where that came from. Maybe our Godtalk inspired me.

"Only one that I know of. It's an ancient method of brewing beer prior to the use of hops. According to tradition, the plant is put in a muslin bag and inserted into a beer barrel. I don't know that it was consumed though. The practice of using it in beer making ended in England sometime in the fifteenth century."

"Does anyone here market a beer using Ivy during the fermentation process?" Depending on his answer, beer labels were about to receive a lot more scrutiny before I bought any again.

"You can't buy beer like that anymore. At least not here. You're safe. It's an unstable product. Even if you wanted to make your own beer, there are far better ways to go about it than using ground ivy. Today, ground ivy would serve merely for ceremonial historical purposes I would think."

Pagan rituals came to mind. I wondered if Carl was thinking the same thing.

CHAPTER 11

Coffee and donut hour at the Clubhouse. I agreed to bring the goodies only because Lori says I should mingle with other members. So, okay, to the donut part anyway. Her parting words resonating, *'You won't meet Mr. Right if you're always in flight.'* I felt sure Mr. Wrong was all I would find here. It takes a special breed to live in an isolated environment like this one. I've asked myself on several occasions if I really would want to mix it up with someone just like me. Probably not. But, since I had the donuts for the weekly event, I had to go. Lori's good.

I opened the door to the smell and warmth of a crackling wood fire inside the lodge building. The look of surprise by my fellow members caught me off guard. Was I that much of an enigma? Then, I realized it was the donut boxes that grabbed their attention. I'd gone all out. When Carl and I ended our meeting with Pastor Mike, I buzzed back up the freeway north to Tacoma Mall's Krispy Kreme. Showing off, I know. Trying to impress? Maybe.

Twenty-five of us made short order of the four dozen assortment in no time. When the clock struck eleven, I figured I could easily slip out. After all, I had a murder to solve.

Arriving at Carl's office, I wondered if I had my wires crossed.

Was I expected? With days running together, and not sleeping all that well, I couldn't be sure where I was supposed to be or when.

Carl raised his eyes from his desk as I entered his office. "Reading *my* mind now or are you sleep walking?"

"Not a mind reader. Though, maybe I am. Should I be here? You don't look like you were expecting me." I left out any reference to recent sleeping patterns.

"No and yes. The case is eating up my budget, but I need you here. I really was about to call you to see if you could come in."

"We had so many new pieces to this puzzle yesterday; I don't know where we are. How's it looking to you today?" I took a seat at the conference table.

"To continue your puzzle reference, I think we have the border mostly connected. Still, there's a lot of the middle that continues to evade us. Just hope we haven't branched off to the point the whole thing goes spilling off the edges."

His frown prompted another movie reference. "Well now, *'Stuff's getting better',* to quote Kevin Costner." I had a good feeling about the day. However, that was no excuse for referencing *anything* from that movie.

"You have the clearer vision this morning, even though your taste in movies is questionable." He came around from behind his desk over to the conference table. Taking a seat next to me with a stack of papers in his hand, he dropped them, with a ceremonial plop, in front of me. "Perhaps today's the day we land a break. You can start by sorting through missing persons' reports."

"Yikes," was all I could muster. "That looks like a couple hundred sheets of paper."

"Some of them are more than one page reports. So, it may not be as bad as it looks."

I spent the next hour examining them while Carl worked at his desk. When I finished, he went to his white board and pulled in a portable board next to it for our work today. "Didn't want to lose our earlier work, so I brought in another board for your vision work."

Hmmm. I thought. One he could erase without damage to his own theory, huh. I was not to be discouraged. "Ready when you are."

"Let's go," he said grabbing a red marker. "Shoot."

"Okay. By States then. Three columns."

The desk phone rang and he held up a finger for me to wait while he scooted around to answer. He finished the call and came back to the board. I tipped my head in the direction of the phone. I could have just asked.

"Shutting down surveillance at the Mounds. With the Holiday weekend over, Seems we can't justify keeping a team stationed there any longer. Have to leave the Preserve security to Ranger Dan and his bosses."

This decision must have come from his boss upstairs, the elected County Sheriff. I doubted Carl would have made the call to pull his team out before he'd caught the murderer. I said, "Ranger Dan could end up a hero after all."

Not pleased with that scenario, he said, "Let's get back to the board, shall we?"

"Sure. First off is Oklahoma. I looked this group over again while you were on the phone, and I think we can narrow it down. I'll give you names of missing young men living within fifty miles of a mound area and the nearest urban center."

"You're using the approximate distance Jake was found in our mounds from the nearest large population center as your mile marker?"

"Roughly, yes." Unpinning my mound areas map from the file, "Here we go. Two lived within reasonable distance of mounds fields and urban centers."

Carl wrote the names under Oklahoma as he asked, "How many does that leave outside the fifty mile radius?"

I counted. "That leaves us with twelve others. Let's start with these and see if my theory pans out. And, to keep your budget for labor costs down." I meant that last part about the budget to come out humorously, but Carl's nod told me it was becoming a concern. I pulled out an atlas from Carl's bookcase.

"Let's go with Tulsa as the population center. Although there's Bartlesville and Muskogee, too."

Carl pulled out his Counties' directory. "I gotta go through each of the sheriff's jurisdiction now, or I'll be in hot water." He flipped through pages making notes on the two missing person's records as he did. "There are three counties we have to go through. All right, keep going."

"Next is Wyoming. Five guys we should look at within that fifty mile radius."

Carl wrote down names as I called them out. Looking over the map of mounds areas and the atlas for the State of Wyoming, I settled on one urban area. "Go with the County around Rock Springs." I added, "Don't ask how many are left, Carl." I hope I didn't sound bossy or snippy. "I want to look at the best possibilities to start, okay?"

I knew Carl was struggling with my approach. His investigation process is far more methodical. His would have resulted in going through all the files to find a connection.

Carl flipped through pages and came up with one County. "This county covers Rock Springs and Green River. I'll go with that."

I continued. "Colorado. Let's look into these eight." I waved them at him. "Gives us a total for the three states of fifteen."

"I'd like to cut that down. Fifteen is going to involve a lot of time when we don't know there will be any positive outcome."

I studied mounds areas and atlas page for Colorado trying to narrow the search area down to one or two cities. It wasn't working. "Too much wilderness and too many mountains in the areas these mounds are located and too many cities running the entire State, north to south. I can't narrow this down to a workable number. Let's put a hold on Colorado for now and work with the other two."

I read off the eight missing person names, and he listed them under Colorado to pursue if results from the first two states warranted it.

"I'll take these seven records for Wyoming and Oklahoma out to Bill to start contacting the County sheriffs' offices. See what we can learn about their disappearance including your big question: Did their moms die on Christmas Eve or thereabouts? I'm thinking I'll have him ask if they were only children, too, like Jake."

"Good idea. Let's also ask what kind of work they did and if they ever served in the Army."

"Those are the big ones. Except whether they had any dealings with the Wiccans."

"Throwing that one in, or at least asking about their faith, covers our whole group of possible suspects," I said pointing to our original white board list.

Tom came in. "Sorry, boss. No callbacks from Connors. He's not answering his phone, either. Want me to contact the hotel people?"

"Not yet. Let's give them the day to get back to us."

It was after three. Carl walked Tom out and both went to Bill's desk to go through the next step: phone calls to county officials in Oklahoma and Wyoming for the select group of seven missing young men. We had worked straight through the afternoon.

Carl looked at his watch when he returned to his office. "Why don't we call it a day? How 'bout I take you to dinner. We'll start where we left off with Scott Connors, construction dirt, and missing persons' reports tomorrow, after we take a much-needed break. Okay with you?"

"Sounds nice. You think we can actually have dinner and not talk about this case?"

"Yes. I'm sure."

Clear and decisive. "I'll go change clothes. Where to?"

"Anthony's Homeport sound good to you?"

"Now, you're reading my mind. Another long time favorite." I picked up my bag and we left, Carl closing his office door behind us.

"Pick you up at five?"

"Sounds great." The elevator doors closed behind me with Carl taking a seat on Bill's desk to review the list of now typed questions that would be part of the next stage of our missing persons' follow-ups.

I flew home, mind whirling on what I had hanging, and clean, in the closet as suitable girl clothes for a dinner date. Did I say '*date*'? Well, dinner out, anyway. It's been forever since I dined in a nice restaurant with a dinner partner, even if he was my work partner. It didn't matter.

*　　*　　*

Arriving ahead of our reservation, the host escorted us to the bar. I tried not to lead. He asked if I liked martinis.

"Would love either a lemon drop or a cosmo." Girly drinks. So what? Tonight I was '*girly*' and it showed. I chose my soft blue silk blouse and tailored navy slacks. I put them together with open toed dress shoes. I even accessorized with a navy clutch. Jewelry, I don't do.

Carl smiled at my drink choice and said, "That surprises me. But, I like it. You look great, by the way."

He ordered a vodka martini, dirty, made with olive brine. Halfway through my drink, I got the vodka giggles. Not the first time. He smiled. I couldn't talk him into answering the riddle about good coffee and good women, hard as I tried.

We ordered a bottle of wine with dinner, red at my request, a mellow Pinot Noir. I was mid way through my tempera salmon and chips when he asked, "Why did you choose mediation and not counseling? And, that's not a work or case question in case you're keeping track."

It was and it wasn't work related, but I wasn't going to nitpick. He was buying, after all. "I considered a counseling career, but, when I did the pros and cons of both, mediation won out big time." I thought about how much detail I wanted to cover tonight and decided on a short version. "Counseling involves long term relationships with people who probably shouldn't be together; or, it involves screwed up kids because of parents who shouldn't have been together." I sounded relationship challenged. Before I could defend my response, he offered his take.

"We've worked several cases now. See each other darn near every day, sometimes for months at a time. You think that's not a relationship? I know you can do relationships."

"It's still a working relationship, Carl. On a non-professional level, we are different people with different backgrounds. For instance, you come from a family consisting of two parents and one child. In many circles, no parenting challenges are associated with that mix. Challenges come with the ability to balance multiple family member needs when there's not enough time, energy, means, or interest to go around. I come from the latter. Throw in sprinkles of illnesses, injuries, drama, and a few tragedies; and, the whole thing can unravel right before your eyes. How that affected my career choice is that entrenching myself in family dysfunction was not where I wanted to spend my working hours nor what I wanted to do for a living."

Carl sat quietly, listening, and hadn't walked out, yet, so I continued.

"Mediation, on the other hand, offers a positive environment for problem solving, giving mostly immediate solutions to single issues. That I can do. It's like the difference between someone wanting to be an emergency room doctor versus a family practitioner. See the difference?"

He said he did.

"Now I have a question for you."

He leaned forward with his chin in his hands. I did the same.

"Tell me again how your name came to be '*Carlton Eugene Watson*'."

He laughed at the sudden change in direction.

We finished our meal, our wine, our dessert, and our coffee. All flavored with stories of the places we've been and the things we've seen along life's journey.

And, not one mention of murder or murderers.

CHAPTER 12

I woke up in a troubled state of mind. Something hovered just out of reach, nagging at me. It was behind a curtain, waiting for me to grab hold of the cord and pull it into the light of day, but I couldn't. Worse, I woke with an irritating urge to call Pastor Mike. For what reason? I didn't know that either.

I worked through two cups of dark bean coffee to clear out the cobwebs. I hoped the urge to pick up the phone would clear out, too. Last night's dinner with Carl had me asking myself, 'Why did I wake up with Pastor Mike on my mind?' I gave myself a stern talking to: *'Don't sabotage this. Stop it.'* Though I refused to say it aloud, I knew what I meant. Am I pushing memories of last night out to keep from giving them a place in my heart?

Taking action to put my mind on anything else, I decided hard labor was a good solution. It's worked before. I reached for the vacuum cleaner and dust cloth. Half an hour later, the house was spotless, but my mind was still dusty. I moved to Plan B. I cleaned the windows.

Sometime later, impressed with what clear shiny windows bring to my mood, the film encompassing my thoughts remained unchanged. I sat down hard and said, "You either call Pastor Mike, hope for the answer when he picks up the phone, or you start ironing." Anything but Plan C.

I went for the phone book. Searching the yellow pages with thousands of church entries, I found Christian Hope. I patted myself on the back for having a good memory for building names, at least, and punched in the number. He picked up on the third ring.

"Good morning, Mike Gordon here."

"Pastor Mike," I began apologetically, "It's Lynzee Rose, Carl's friend?"

"Of course. An unexpected pleasure to hear from you."

"Listen. This is going to sound crazy, but I've had some sort of omen that I'm supposed to call you, only I don't know why."

"Omen?" Pastor Mike remained silent for a couple of minutes and then said, "Tell me how this came about. From the beginning."

Working hard not to sound like I was in confession, I went through my night's wakeful and dreamlike hours and the lingering feelings about something waiting to be discovered.

"Okay. Let's start with *why* this morning."

"Alright. I'm thinking the dreams, or whatever they were, happened because I had a great night out and my tired brain took a night off, too." Even I had to admit that sounded ridiculous. "Other than that, it's Wednesday, just another Wednesday, and an unsolved case, and I'm talking to you, for some reason. Nothing else is special about today or tomorrow, for that matter." Long pause. "Hello?" Were we disconnected?

"Lynzee, I think what happened for you last night is that your prayers were answered."

Darn it. This was not why I called.

I was about to protest when he added, "About the case, I mean."

Whew. I'd almost ended the call. "How so?" I didn't pray for anything that I could remember.

"I believe you had a vision, similar to when God spoke to Daniel in dreams. But, not having Daniel's ability to interpret dreams, I can only tell you, by your overwhelming need to call me, that God directed you to me."

"What are you talking about?" My voice rose in frustration.

"I'm talking about the curtain that's been keeping you from seeing the answers you've been after. He had no other way to help you understand. He steered you to me. And, what's behind that curtain has everything to do with today and tomorrow."

I still thought he was talking about saving my soul, but I gave him the benefit of my doubts, for the moment. Calmly, I asked, "What about today and tomorrow?"

"You'd better sit down. I think you just cracked your case wide open."

I was sitting down, but I understood his meaning. I took a deep breath and readied myself.

"Tomorrow is Ascension Day."

I was half way out of my chair as the words hit. "Tell me it has something to do with ground ivy and beer." I could see the dots starting to connect right before my eyes.

"I think you and Carl better head over. I'll call him while you drive yourself. You know how to find us, right?"

"I remember. See you in a few."

My head was spinning, my heart was pumping madly, and I didn't know what to make of what my brain was doing. The curtain was opening and with it, the fog was lifting. I was all over the place. I spun around looking for sensible shoes, keys and everything else that goes with getting out the door in a hurry.

They were standing outside, waiting for me. Carl immediately headed out to me with a look of concern, he put his arm around me as we walked, almost propping me up. "Are you okay? Mike said you had quite the revelation."

I wasn't going to argue about Mike's choice of words, nor the assistance Carl gave me now as we passed Jesus going into the building. The truth be known, I was still shaken.

The building was abuzz with activity. We headed down the hallway with rooms full of people busying about in all modes of preparations. I wondered if it had something to do with Ascension Day.

We took seats in Mike's office as he closed the door. "We have our food bank here today; it's going to get loud and crazy soon."

Oh.

He went to his chair behind the desk and sat with his arms resting on the handrails, his hands clasped in prayerful pose. We waited. He took a moment and then, "In a nutshell, Ascension Day celebrates the day that Christ, in the presence of His Apostles, ascended *bodily* into Heaven. Ascension Day occurs on the fortieth day of Easter, so it falls on a Thursday, this Thursday to be exact."

My mind was racing again. "That's why the killer took the bones from the morgue. He wants to put them back in the ground before tomorrow." Still thinking about the ground ivy, I added, "And beer?"

Carl started to object, his mind processing that I might be off subject.

I glanced over at him and finished my sentence properly. "I'm asking if the ground ivy in beer is part of Ascension Day festivities. Somewhere."

He nodded, mostly in relief.

We turned back to Pastor Mike. "I did a little internet surfing while I was waiting for you both to arrive. Every year in Oxford, crowds drink specially brewed ale, prepared with ground ivy, as part of the Day's celebrations. Other activities involve a procession of people for what's called a '*beating of the bounds*' ceremony. It has to do with establishing the boundaries of the local parish. Today, you'll find a slight modification to another tradition; that of throwing fired pennies to children. The idea of this practice was to see which children would go after the coins even if it meant they would burn their hands picking them up. I tell you all of this so you have the full feel of the earlier times celebration. How much of this information has to do with the case, I'll leave to you. That covers Ascension Day celebrations in a snapshot."

"They are God's tear drops." Both men turned in their seats half expecting I was having another omen, or vision, as it were. Maybe I was. "I took another look at the aerial picture. It's a stretch, but mounds do have a tear shaped appearance to them. God's teardrops, remember, Carl? "

"I remember you mentioning something about it. But, honestly, I thought you were on the trail of the alien chasers, so I didn't put much thought on it, Carl said apologetically. "And, I thought that tear shaped business was a localized story."

"I don't know for sure that it is. I do know the killer is going back to the Mounds to rebury those bones. I know it as I know my own name."

"Then we've got our day cut out for us. Back to my office."

Thanking Pastor Mike as we hurried out, this time *I* gave the Pastor a hug, not to anyone's surprise.

Carl was rifling through a good-sized stack of messages and papers when I walked in. Picking up his phone as I stopped in front of his desk, he smiled into the phone saying, "Tom? Would you bring Bill and come in, please."

Less than thirty seconds later, he announced, "Gentlemen, our first real lead in cracking this case comes from our own Lynzee Rose."

To say I blushed, is an understatement. My face matched the fuchsia blouse I'd thrown on. I now regretted that choice. I sat down.

Both eyed us suspiciously.

Unfazed, Carl continued, "Our killer is here and about to rebury those bones in the Mounds."

Their eyes popped open, jaws dropping, as he filled them in on our meeting with Pastor Mike. He took a deep breath and began outline what lay ahead for us. "The trouble is we don't know exactly when our target will show up. My best guess is it's going to go down sometime after the Mounds close for the night."

Bill and Tom took a seat at the table as Carl ushered them further into his office. He closed the door and joined us.

He held up a finger as he said, "Problem one, we moved the dirt out of the original burial site. That puts the entire Preserve at play. Problem two, our presence must be inconspicuous. Problem three, we only have today to put together a plan to monitor the fields with the fewest number of personnel involved." He looked back and forth at Bill and Tom, wiggling his fingers for emphasis. "I need a plan we can bounce around, say in about an hour?"

They exited excitedly to the first empty room they could find where they could spread out maps and photos and put together their ideas.

Carl smiled. "We should go out more often. Look what happened!"

I smiled back, at his complement and the memory of our evening, still at a loss for words. And, I was feeling an exhilarating high, unfamiliar for me.

Carl wasn't at a loss for words. He went to his desk and rifled through more messages, papers, and files. He walked back and sat back down at the table. "Now, let's see what all we have here that might help us narrow all this down some, starting with the dirt, shall we?"

He was being lighthearted even though we had a heavy day ahead of us. I liked it.

"Some of the construction dirt went to a local senior center garden project, another batch to the Boys and Girls Club for a grass seeding project, but," he stopped to emphasize the next entry on the list, "most of it went to Ft. Lewis-McChord Base, project listed as classified."

"How about that," I finally dragged out. My words were starting to come back. "Puts the Army unit right back in the mix. It would be a perfect day if the dirt was the right dirt, too."

He flipped through sheets of paper, separating out pink message slips as he did. "Got it right here. Doc marked it as an 'urgent request'. He handed me the report sheet, keeping an eye on what my reaction would be.

I took the report drawing in a deep breath as I read, *'The construction site topsoil is consistent with the soil brought into Mima Mounds.'* Wanting to jump to my feet and give a loud high five *'yes,'* I settled for, "I can't believe it. All of a sudden, the dots are all connecting, the tumblers are lining up, the pieces coming together. We're going to catch this son of a ......" I stopped short of saying it.

From the look on his face, he wouldn't have minded. Flashing a pink message slip at me, he said, "Seems we can meet with Scott as long as there is a company attorney present. So, we have to go attorney to attorney. The higher ups here won't permit a one sided legal showdown. You know how much time we'll lose putting that together?"

I think I did. "It's not going to happen today. Let's focus on a killer profile. I'm thinking our most likely suspect is either Scott, some Army guy or gal, or an unknown serial killer." I'd said it out loud. The *"S"* word now out there in the universe."

"What about Brooke?"

"The construction site dirt give away moves her down my list. I don't picture her involved with Boys and Girls Clubs, or senior center garden projects, do you? And, she has an alibi for when the bones were taken."

From the corner of my eye, I saw Bill hustling toward his desk where an old man stood, hat in hand. Bill appeared to know who it was. He stammered trying to decide between Carl's office and the chair next to his desk, all in one motion. It hit me. "Oh my God, Carl, it's Ralph. Ralph Connors is out there!"

On his feet, he sprinted out of his office. I watched him speak to both briefly. Then, Bill led Ralph down the hall. Returning, clasping his hands behind his head, he looked up at the ceiling and said, "He wants to report Scott as missing. You ready for this?"

I wasn't sure I was, but I was on my feet and out the door before I'd finished the thought.

The three of us sat staring at each other. Since icebreakers is supposed to be my specialty, I started. "Ralph, what's happened?

You don't look well. Are you all right? Would you like a drink of water?"

On cue, Carl was up out of his seat and back with a bottle of water. He placed it in front of Ralph.

We waited while Ralph drank a good portion. Then, rotating the bottle between his palms as he gathered his thoughts, he began his story. I'm sorry to be such a bother. You all have been so nice to me. I didn't know what to do or where else to go."

Looking for confirmation that he'd chosen correctly in coming here, I smiled and reached out to squeeze his hand. He relaxed and continued.

"As you know, Miss Rose, I haven't had much contact with my son, Scott, for a several days. I started thinking about this young lad found in the Mounds. It made me think of Scott. Their build and looks are similar. I got worried something bad had happened to him, too."

Carl was all business. "Mr. Connors, has Scott been missing over forty-eight hours?"

Ralph had more than reason for coming here today. I interjected before he could answer, "Ralph, we're here to help you. Let's start at the beginning. I asked, "Scott lost his mother and you your wife, what four, five years ago, was it?"

"Yes ma'am. We've been without Gretchen for five years now."

Suddenly dawning on me, "Why are there no pictures of her, or your son, hanging in your home?" Dysfunction, with a capital "D," was calling and answering heavily on my shoulders.

"Scott took them down. Said it was too painful. He took away most of the pictures of himself with his mother a few years back."

"How did she die, if you don't mind my asking?"

"One night, Christmas Eve it was, Gretchen just looked at us, closed her eyes, smiled, and stopped breathing. They said her heart gave out."

I felt like I was going to lose last night's meal. My stomach tightened into a knot.

Carl looked better than I did, but pale all the same. He leaned into the table and asked, "Is there something you're not telling us, has something happened?"

I whipped around in Carl's direction. What did I miss?

Ralph lowered his head, ashamed. "Scott stopped by Monday morning. Told him how you all have been stopping by to check on me from time to time. I wanted him to feel bad for ignoring me, I guess. It was wrong. I started to ask him about some of the missing tools when he started yelling about not being the 'Perfect Son' I wanted and how his mother was the only one that loved him for who he was. Told me I was the one trying to keep him from being the carpenter he wanted to be. He got so quiet then and just left. I've never seen him like that. I tried calling him, to talk it over, but he's not answering his phone."

I *am* going to be sick, but later.

Carl clenched his jaw and stood up. "Ralph, will you excuse us a minute?"

Ralph was lost in his own misery covering his face in his hands as we stepped out. I'm not sure he even heard us. I kept my eye on the window into the room, worried about his mental state. "Carl, is Scott the one we've been looking for?"

"He grew up next door to Mima Mounds. He would know his way in and out of there blindfolded." Carl continued through a mental checklist on the possibility.

"If he's not the killer, he could be a target. He fits the profile." I looked through the window. Ralph was looking better. "What do we do with Ralph?"

"We need to keep him close by. I don't want him connecting with Scott til we know what we're dealing with."

I had an idea. "Why don't we focus on the missing person's report he said he came in to file? Keep him busy with us until we can think of what to do next."

"Sandy's good with people Ralph's age. I'll fill her in. Tell her to bypass the forty-eight hour requirement, and ask her take her time; be extra patient with him. I'm going to call Pastor Mike next, ask him to clear his calendar, and help Ralph through this ordeal. If we're right about Scott, he's gonna have to draw very hard on his faith to get through this night. Sound like a plan to you?"

"Yeah. Perfect." I couldn't argue with the plan. Carl was right. Sandy looked surprised at the request, but the more Carl briefed her, the more she looked ready for the assignment. He turned toward the room where Ralph was waiting and flipped open his phone. Hand on the doorknob, he snapped it shut up seconds later and went in. Sandy gathered up what she needed and walking quickly, knocked, then disappearing inside.

I sprinted into Carl's office and closed the door. I took a deep breath and tried to relax. No way was I going back in there. No way.

A few minutes later, the office door opened. He peeked in. "Okay if I join you?"

"I'm sorry. I'm sick about this. Poor Ralph. The whole family. It's, it's awful. I can't go back in there."

"Hey. Don't be sorry. You earned your stripes today. Remember?"

"Yeah. Okay. I'll be fine."

"I know you will. I'm going out to brief Bill and Tom on what's happened and see what they've come up with for a plan."

His real intent was to brief them away from where I was, giving me more time to pull myself together. Good on him. Now, I needed to do the work in the few minutes I had. I folded my arms in front of me on the table and rested my head, closing my eyes.

It wasn't long before the three of them walked in. They were talking about Scott. They decided to put out a BOLO for his truck. The instructions, they decided, would be not to engage but to call in if they spotted him. Carl went to his desk and made the call.

I picked up Scott's file. Not much to it. I studied the picture we downloaded from the Hotel web page. Something about his face was familiar. I'd seen him before. "Carl." The three of them turned from where they had gathered around Carl's desk. I spun the file around pointing to the picture of Scott Connors.

"I've seen him. Even talked to him, well he talked to me actually."

Carl's confused look told me I best get all my words back fast.

"It was Saturday. He was at the Mounds."

Bill's eye's opened wide.

I was feeling light-headed and my skin was feeling creepy-crawly. "It was Ranger Dan's tour group. They walked by me. I was standing in front of the recently removed mound."

Carl turned to Bill who stood stone like. Not wanting to get Bill in hot water for letting me wander around with our now top suspect in arms reach, I caught Bill's eye. "He was the last guy in the group. He walked right passed, muttering."

Bill grateful for the save, gave an affirmative nod to Carl.

"The guy said something like, '*disturbing the peace*' or something along those lines. I didn't pay much attention to him. I thought he was talking about the new mound being there as the *disturbing* part. Now, I'm thinking he meant we disturbed the peace removing it."

Carl spun around. "Tom. Bill. About the out of state missing persons' search we're doing, put a hold on them for now. Once we have our suspect in custody tonight," he pounded his fist into his palm repeatedly, "I'll find out if there are more buried bodies we should be looking for."

The three of us sat stunned, imagining Carl's implied interview strategy. Perhaps it was time to return to finalizing a plan. "What *is* our strategy for capturing the suspect?" I put emphasis on the word '*capturing*'.

We huddled together, listening to Bill and Tom's ideas, until we finalized the best plan we could in the time available. One involving the fewest active players. One that protects Ralph and all of us. And, one that insures we'd have Scott, or whoever it turned out to be if it wasn't Scott, in custody, alive.

We broke for lunch and agreed to meet in Carl's office at three. A bowl of pasta had my name on it. I headed out the door to find it.

Pastor Mike exited the elevator as I approached, his eyes focused straight ahead. I watched as Sandy, Pastor Mike, and Ralph Connors entered Carl's office. They were about to break the news of our suspicions and encourage Ralph to best help Scott by helping us. I did not envy Carl that task. Talk about broken hearts. I pushed the elevator button, stepped inside and held the door as I watched Ralph's face change from concern to fear and then to despair. I released the elevator door and burst into tears.

*   *   *

Carl signed out two unmarked cars from the motor pool. No flashing red lights for this night. While I was at lunch, he briefed his boss and assembled two teams. I knew he wouldn't be thinking about food, so I brought him an Italian meatball sandwich.

Bill drove off in Ralph's car with another officer seated in the front seat. I didn't recognize him.

Detective Sandy Jackman exited the parking lot in one of the motor pool cars. Ralph sat in the back seat with Pastor Mike. This group was on its way to Ralph's home, for the duration. They would unplug the house phone. Not having a cell phone would resolve Ralph trying to contact his son in some moment of regret. Scott would find he was not able to reach his dad by phone. Would that be reason enough for him to drive to his childhood home? Maybe. And finally, only Ralph's car would be parked in front of the house. Most of the house lights and the porch and yard lights would be left on; extra visibility for the team and a beacon of curiosity for Scott if he came around. The County car would be parked behind the barn.

The next team consisted of Carl, Tom, and me. We rode in the second motor pool car. Carl finished his sandwich as we left the parking lot. Sufficiently warned I was a civilian and, technically, shouldn't be involved at this stage of an operation, I made it clear with one look they could take me with them or have me drive my bright red Transit into the Preserve parking lot. They chose wisely.

We arrived at the Mounds parking lot, and stashed our vehicle from view. Tom grabbed the key ring from the office. The three of us jumped into the truck with Ranger Dan. He locked the gate behind us. We drove out down the two-lane County road, and took a right into the small campfire area on the North edge of the Preserve.

Dan pulled out a pair of bolt cutters and set about releasing the fence section. The goal was to make the fence appear the same as it looked in December. We would wait here. Our plan assumed the killer would use the same entry spot as the first time. We had no other ideas, so we went with what we knew.

Carl told Ranger Dan to leave the area and not return unless we called. Relief showed on his face. Confronting killers was not in his job description.

We took cover in a patch of sword ferns, smushing them enough to give us a place to wait and watch unseen. Talking, I was told, was ill advised. I passed the time thinking about Scott. If he was the killer, what possessed this local farm boy turned architect turned construction worker to turn into this? On the ride down, Carl told me the question I should be asking wasn't 'what' but 'who' possessed him. *"Potatoes, Putahtoes,"* I responded.

A said a silent prayer for our side. It couldn't hurt. It was new to me, but it came easy enough. *'Please, God, let this be the only one.'* Deciding even God can't change what's already occurred, I made a quick revision and added, *'Or, please let this end here now.'*

Letting my prayer stand on its own, I went back to my thoughts. If Scott is killing young men like himself, men who lost their mothers on Christmas Eve, why? Ralph told us Scott felt he wasn't perfect enough for him, but believed he had been where his mother was concerned. Was he sacrificing perfect young men for his mother? Why had he not offering himself instead? And, what about this Ascension Day aspect? Does he believe these young men will be lifted up into Heaven? For his mother to have her perfect son? All fine questions but none I could answer. Only the killer had the answers to why.

Our plan included making contact on the hour. The time had come. Tom got up, moving away from our location, to check in with the Connors' farm team. I jumped up, albeit not very quietly. I was shushed immediately. I whispered, "Let me go; you two stay here. I gotta go." It was clear what I meant. We hadn't factored in nature calls that included a female on the stakeout. One that wanted a restroom and not a tree to squat behind. Oh, well. Best laid plans.

"Are you serious? You live in the middle of nature and you won't use it when nature calls?" Carl's whispered voice was gaining volume.

"Sorry. No can do. Never could," my whisper matching his volume. I crossed my arms to make it clear I wasn't going anywhere but to the restroom.

Carl came up with a plan to meet all our needs. He would stay on location behind the ferns. I would make the check-in call from inside the restroom building and then come back, quietly he reminded me. Tom would show me how to reach Bill on the radio, give me the restroom key, walk me to the restroom, then go back to the path and wait between Carl's location and where he could still see the restroom. The restroom wasn't located out in the Mound's field. Carl's plan met his requirement to keep both me and the stakeout safe.

Armed with a quick lesson on how to raise Bill on the radio, I left with it and the restroom key. Tom double-checked that he had the gate and office key. Satisfied we had everything we needed, we started off.

We arrived with no trouble. The path was well defined. It was still light enough to find our way. And, it was dark enough for me to be camouflaged in Carl's dark jacket. I remembered not to turn on the flashlight I borrowed from Carl until I was inside the restroom. I finished up and made the check-in call. All was quiet on the home front at the farm.

I locked up behind me and started down the path. I saw Tom standing on the path up ahead. I took a few more steps in his direction and waved. Then, I heard something. Or did I? I stopped walking and turned my head in the direction of the sound. I did hear something.

Tom pulled out his binoculars to get a better look at why I had stopped moving. I used big hand gestures to tell him to come to me, my hand on my ear to let him know I heard noises, and my arm pointing to where I thought it was coming from.

He put up his hand to say stop and wait then jogged off to get Carl. Unfortunately, my interest was in getting out of the open. I tiptoed back to the restroom. I wanted to radio Carl. I didn't know how to call his radio. Something we didn't plan or, my having to radio Carl. Think, Lynzee. Ah yes, my cell phone. I used auto dial. Carl answered on the first ring, annoyed he hadn't put it on vibrate.

"Lynzee, what are you doing," he whispered loudly.

Tom obviously had not made it back to tell Carl about my hand gestures.

I whispered into my phone, "There's something happening over on this side of the Mounds. Tom's on his way back to you. There's a noise. Not where we are. The area closer to the entrance road. I think we're in the wrong spot."

He whispered loudly again, "Wait right where you are. I'm on my way to you. We'll check it out. Tom will stay at this location with my radio in case it's still going down here."

"I'm in the restroom. I guarantee you I'm not going anywhere til you knock on the door." I hung up.

A few minutes later I heard a *'tap, tap'* on the door. I wish I'd told him to give some secret knock. It could be anyone out there.

"Lynzee, you in there? It's Carl. Open up," he said in hushed tones.

Relieved in more than one way now, I opened the door.

He put his fingers to his lips and gave me the *'quiet'* sound.

I handed him his flashlight and stepped out, taking my place, right behind him. I'm no hero, of that I was suddenly very aware. Shaking, a combination of the cool evening air and my own fear, we started walking across the parking lot and onto the main trail. The sound started again. I started to say something. He stopped me.

"I hear it. Stay close."

Absolutely, I thought.

Through the darkness settling on the prairie, the scraping sound continued to echo faintly. We walked the paved trail, our steps soundless. We came to the unpaved section. It split off from the main path.

The sound stopped suddenly. I put my hand on Carl's shoulder for him to stop moving. We listened together. Nothing. What to do? Which way to go? Taking the dirt path would make our approach easier to be overheard by whoever it was out there. Should we stay on the paved path? It intersected the gravel path further on. My mind raced again. We had to make a decision and fast.

I stepped in front of Carl and held out my hand to tell him to give me a minute. I closed my eyes, putting myself in the killer's mindset. What would I do if I were in a hurry, trying to meet a deadline to get Jake in the right place at the right time? This time, the answer did not hide behind a curtain. It was right in front of me.

I took a hard left off trail, building to a run, into the section of mounds we'd visited with Ranger Dan, the section that included the mound sliced open for examination years and years ago. I picked up speed. Carl started after me.

Instinct drove me forward. I dropped to my knees in front of what had been the cutaway mound only days ago. I clawed at fresh dirt crying, "No. No. No."

Carl came to a halt behind me, trying to take in what he was seeing but not understanding; then, fully understanding. He yelled into his radio, "Tom, get over here. I'll throw up a flare. Watch yourself. I don't know what all we got. I don't think we should assume we're alone." He turned his flashlight on and scanned the area, gun drawn. We were vulnerable.

He turned his flashlight on me; it's beam inadequate. He slapped at it, hoping for more light. He radioed Bill at the Connor farm and told him to come to where the flares were going up. He told him to leave the other two officers behind with Ralph and Pastor Mike and to stay alert.

The flares hit the sky. My hearing numbed with the sudden light. I tuned out all sounds, everything suddenly moving in slow motion. I continued clawing at the dirt. I felt something and grabbed at it, pulling it toward me. Startled as I registered what I was holding, I dropped it then scrambled back and picked up the lifeless hand again. I sobbed, crying out, No. Don't do this. No." I scrambled backward, pulling and pulling.

Tom was on us, breathless from his run across the field. Carl directed him in my direction. He dropped to where I crouched, and without a word, he began pulling at the dirt, throwing it side to side and up and down. Anywhere to get it off whoever was under it.

I don't know how much time went by, but when I could focus and hear again, I found myself seated on the tailgate of an ambulance, seemingly not far from where my last memory was, Carl picking me up off the ground.

I could now hear myself speaking, "I'm fine. Really." I was crying.

Carl put his arm around me. I tried to breathe normally. We didn't speak again until my tears had stopped. I looked up at Carl trying to gather my thoughts.

He gave me a wink. "You saved his life. They're bringing him over now. Come on. Let's move you away from this."

I stood up and walked away from the ambulance activity. Carl steered me toward the county vehicles, headlights now lighting the fields.

"Who, Carl?"

The attendants approached, pushing and pulling their load across the rough terrain. I craned my neck to see. Someone was strapped to the stretcher. An oxygen mask covered the face. I wanted to know who it was. I needed to know.

Then, behind the stretcher and climbing into the ambulance was Pastor Mike. After him, Ralph and Sandy got in. The ambulance took off, siren blaring.

Now the blank spot in my memory of the last minutes started to fill in. I turned pointing in the direction of the exposed mound. "It was Scott then?"

Carl spoke softly, "It was. It is."

"Tell me, please."

"Are you sure you're up to it, Lynzee. I'm worried about you."

"Please, Carl."

"Okay. Stop me if you need a break. Here's what happened. You and Tom managed to locate him and pull him out. Scott was clutching the black bag, the one we saw leave the morgue. Jake's remains, we assume, are inside."

"And Scott?"

He'd inhaled a lot of dirt, but we got him breathing again. He's not out of the woods yet, but I think he'll make it."

"How?"

Not certain I wasn't in shock, Carl readjusted the blanket around my shoulders. *"How* what? Are you sure you want to do this now?"

"Tell me everything." I looked him in the eye. "Please."

"We found his truck nearby. Looks like he's been living in it the past few days, maybe all week. I don't know. We'll know more after he's well enough to talk to, physically that is. He's going to need a real good lawyer, and an even better therapist."

"Don't look at me!"

He saw through my comic relief. I gave a half smile, tired after the emotional rollercoaster and adrenalin rush now in its downhill slide.

"His toolbox was behind the driver's seat of his truck. And, to answer your yet to be asked question, yes, he had a scratch awl. Bagged and tagged it. Looks like we can return the stuff we collected from Brian the other day.

Somehow, that didn't make me feel any better. Carl continued.

"Found the camping shovel he was using underneath all the dirt you two were throwing around. That was the scraping sound. There are half a dozen plastic five-gallon buckets nearby. Looks like he'd been coming in after hours, scooping out the mound, and transferring the dirt Ranger Dan conveniently dumped."

I nodded quickly encouraging him to continue.

"He dug out a deep hole and climbed in with Jake's remains.

I shivered at the vision.

Carl watched me to see if I'd tuned out again. I hadn't. He continued.

"He had it rigged so's the dirt would collapse around and on top of him once he got far enough in. He pulled at the dirt and got enough in to cover himself.."

"So, he did it, then? I saved the life of a murderer?" I suddenly found myself at a crossroad.

Carl grabbed me by the shoulders and leaned down, peering into my eyes. "You saved the life of a man, Lynz. It's not for us to decide who lives and who dies. You did the right thing. A hard thing, but the right thing. Jesus died for Barabbas, too, you know."

"Barabbas? The murderer in the Bible?"

"Yes. Christ died for *all* our sins, whatever our crimes may be."

"Did he say anything?"

"Scott? Yeah. He's not very rational right now. Maybe, he hasn't been in a while. Once we got him breathing regular he kept mumbling about this place being a portal to heaven. Kept telling us to call him *'the carpenter', d*emanding we let him finish his work, saying we were ruining everything. It goes downhill from there."

"It's not Ralph's fault." My heart was breaking for him.

"No. It's not. Both of them dealt with grief and loss in their own way. Neither of them turned to strengthening their relationship with God. May have prevented all of this if they had."

I was suddenly worn out, wanting to go home, crawl under my covers and sleep for a decade.

"Carl, will you drive me back to my car now? I want to go home."

"I wouldn't have it any other way."

EPILOGUE

THURSDAY, JUNE 2ND

Ascension Day

In the days and weeks that followed, the County phones rang off their hooks. The FBI was in, out, and back again. Different state County Sheriff units appeared, disappeared, and reappeared.

Though Scott waived his right to an attorney. My guess is there'd be a bunch of them, and psychiatrists, knocking on the door to represent this disturbed man.

With Pastor Mike's guidance, the truth emerged. We learned Scott was responsible for four deaths, or *'rebirths'* as he called them, all killed on Christmas Eve over a four-year period. Thurston County's Jacob Mathews was the fourth and final such death. We'd stopped him.

Scott added ground ivy to the specially brewed beer he prepared each year for his sacrificial ceremony. He told authorities it cut the taste of the over the counter antihistamines he added to get his victims relaxed. He used his scratch awl to paralyze victims so he could bury them properly. He said it was important for each one to be alive when he covered them. We didn't ask.

Scott Connors' connection with reality tumbled into a downward spiral the moment we interfered with his Ascension Day crusade. Counties in Wyoming, Oklahoma, and Colorado all confirmed finds of the three other missing men, all fitting Jake's general description. The killings might have gone on for years with another victim most certainly scheduled for Burns, Oregon, the site of the next hotel construction site near a field of mounds.

I thanked God my prayer had been answered. It was over.

Jacob Mathews got his full military service. We all attended.

Luke 24:50 - 51 (NIV)
[50] When he had led them out to the vicinity of Bethany,
he lifted up his hands and blessed them.
[51] While he was blessing them,
he left them and was taken up into heaven.

About the Author

A native of the Pacific Northwest, Victoria Walters draws on her extensive problem-solving career, assisted by story developer and son, Seth Williamson, to produce an inspiring new whodunit series.

Set in the South Puget Sound area of Washington State, the setting for her novel series is inlaid with quirky community and natural and manmade local wonders.

Victoria lives in Olympia, Washington, with her Border Collie, Mr. Barky Pants.

Watch for, *Errant Son,* book two in the Lynzee Rose Mystery Series. In this suspenseful installment to *Perfect Son,* Lynzee is back at work in her mediation practice only to be called on to assist her friend and sometimes boss, Detective Carl Watson, to investigate a bizarre discovery at a local and baffling man made wonder, Gospodor Monument Park... a place steeped in its own mystery.